SCOTIA STORMS BOOKS 10-12

CATHRYN FOX

Discover other titles by Cathryn Fox at www.cathrynfox.com. Please sign up for Cathryn's Newsletter for freebies, ebooks, news and contests: https://app.mailerlite.com/webforms/landing/c1f8n1
ISBN ebook : 978-1-998943-43-2
ISBN Print: 978-1-998943-42-5

DEAL BREAKER

Cathryn Fox

1

RHYS

"The girls here definitely aren't like the ones at home," my brother Dane announces as he wags his eyebrows at his best friend, acting like an ass. No way am I putting up with that behavior. I turn to him as he takes in the crowd of sorority girls walking around Storm House, a post-Christmas party in full swing. Of course, it's nothing compared to what the place is going to look like on New Year's Eve—and I'm so goddamn tired of it.

"What's that supposed to mean?" I ask, tipping my cup up to take a sip of beer as I stare at my kid brother, who I've been keeping a close eye on. After Christmas, he and his friend came back to the city with me. They're both attending Scotia Academy next year, and I agreed to let them stay in my dorm room and show them around. But I am so over this partying shit. Thank God I only have one semester left, then it's off to play defense for the Boston Bucks.

Dane snorts. I'm not sure why he feels the need to act like the big man on campus. It pisses me off. "The girls back home are basic, and the girls here are DTF." I smack the side of his head. "What the fuck, Cheddar?" he complains.

"Down to fuck? Really? Have some fucking respect."

He rubs his head and exchanges a strange look with his friend. Yeah, I get it. I have a reputation a mile long and they both know it. But a reputation is one thing. Wild antics and partying is what people expect from me. Over the last four years, I've watched all my friends grow up, and settle down. Damned if I'm not jealous. The only problem is that girls aren't attracted to Rhys Taylor. They all want a piece of Cheddar—a nickname given to me because I have red hair, and because my parents operate the biggest artisan cheese company in Bass River, an hour outside the city.

"I need another drink," Dane mumbles under his breath and nudges his friend Jesse.

"Don't drink too much," I shout out after him.

"Okay, Dad."

I shake my head as he leaves. Maybe my kid brother is trying to impress me, and maybe I am turning into Dad. That makes me laugh. Now I know how Dad feels when he was trying to tame me back in the day. I have to say, my kid brother is definitely following in my footsteps, and I'm not sure that's a good thing. The truth is, I want him to respect women. I might have slept around, sure, and partied as Cheddar, but I'm still Rhys underneath it all, and I treat women the way they should be treated, with respect.

As my brother disappears, my phone pings and I pull it from my back pocket. I take another fast glance around Storm House before I read the message. Even though I still have a room in the frat, I barely know anyone here tonight. I know the players, just not as well as I know the guys from my coming up years. The team has changed over the last four years, taken over by the new kids ready to make their mark in the world. I turn my attention to my phone and my heart beats a little faster as I read the message.

Lisa: Hey Rhys, how's your night going?

Me: Not bad. At Storm House. Keeping an eye on my younger brother. Are you still in Calgary?

Lisa and I have been chatting for weeks now. I'm on an app, and yeah okay, it might be a bit pathetic, but I own that. Seriously though, I wanted to meet someone who didn't know me as Cheddar. Someone who'll call me Rhys and get to know the guy beneath the jersey. Lisa, who I'm chatting with now, went home for the holidays but she goes to college here. We've yet to meet in person, and I'm not in a rush. I like getting to know her like this first.

Lisa: Still here with the fam. You're a good big brother.

Me: I still have a few more days with him and if he keeps talking shit, no one will ever find the body.

Lisa: (Laughing emoji) You're too funny. I won't keep you. Go have fun, but not too much fun. <wink>

Me: I'd rather be talking to you.

Lisa: Such a sweet talker.

I laugh at that. Okay, that might have come off a bit cheesy, but then again, they do call me Cheddar. Lisa doesn't, though, and I want her to think I'm more than a FBOI. Sure, I've always been a fuck boy. Is it so want to want more? I glance up and spot my brother handing Nate's sister Kendra a cup. Shit. Nate will be replacing Caleb as team captain next year when we all graduate and Dane—who will be the new kid on the team—should not be messing with Nate's little sister.

Me: GTG, my brother is about to get himself into a world of hurt.

Lisa: Uh oh. What is he doing?

Me: Looking at Nate's sister like he's DTF.

Lisa: Go, save his butt.

Me: I'll message you later, okay?

Lisa: Sounds good.

Before I tuck my phone away, another message comes in.

Lisa: I'm looking forward to it, and you ARE a good big brother.

I can't seem to wipe the stupid smile off my face as I slide my phone into my back pocket. I really like Lisa, even though I have no idea what she looks like. All I know is she goes to school here and is studying English. She wants to be a writer. I thought about checking with my buddy Brandon to see if he knew her. He's an aspiring writer too, but I kind of like the idea of keeping us in this bubble for now. I like having her all to myself.

I push off the wall and start toward my brother, when a pretty girl I've seen around stumbles into me. I grip her shoulders before she falls and she smiles up at me.

"Cheddar." Her hands go to my chest and she widens her fingers. "Thanks for saving me."

I hold onto her and inch back, afraid she'll fall if I let her go. I glance at her half-closed eyes, trying to place her. I think her name is Leeza, but I'm not sure. I've seen her around campus before. Never at a frat party, though. What is she doing here now?

"Are you okay?" I ask.

She giggles. "I am now."

I lift my head and spot my brother moving in closer to Nate's sister, and that's when I turn and catch the way Nate is staring at them, his brow furrowed. Oh fuck. I need to get to Dane before Nate does, but there's no way I can let go of the girl I'm holding up.

I scan the room, and note the girls on the stairs, some headed up, some headed down. "Where are your friends?" I understand girl code. They come together and check in with one another before they leave.

She waves her hand. "Gone, they all hooked up."

"Did you text them?" She pulls out her phone and waves it in front of my face, too fast for me to see anything. "They're not messaging back. Too busy hooking up."

While I'd like to take her phone and look through it myself, I don't want to invade her privacy. "Come with me." I put my arm around her, and she sags against me.

"Where are we going?"

I push through a few people, and hurry toward Dane. "I need to get my brother." Luckily, I reach him before Nate.

I grab him by the shirt. "Time to go."

He shrugs me off. "What? No. The party is just starting." The girl in my arms hiccups, and my brother gives me a knowing nod. "Ah, I get it."

No, he doesn't get it. You'd think he knew me better than to think I'd take a drunk girl back to my room and fuck her. "I need to get her home."

"I'm not stopping you, bro."

I growl. "Dane—"

"Hey," Nate says pushing in beside me. His sister stands a little straighter, and Nate takes her cup and smells it.

"It's just beer," she says.

Nate takes a drink and hands it back. She rolls her eyes, and I get it. Nate is crazy overprotective of her and I can't blame him. The players on the team have a reputation of sleeping with anyone willing, but he also knows better than to think we'd drug anyone. We're a good bunch of guys, despite the reputation, and it's up to the captain to ensure the new recruits follow the straight and narrow. My brother, however, is my responsibility right now and the opportunity to teach him a lesson is right in the palm of my hand.

"Dane is my brother," I explain, and Nate relaxes.

"Oh, hey man. I heard about you. Looking forward to you being on the team. If you play anything like Cheddar..." Nate pauses and puts his hand on my shoulder. "We're well on our way to winning another season." He pulls Kendra closer to him, a not so subtle indication that she's off limits. My brother is smart enough to pick up the cues he's dropping. At least, I hope he is.

"I need to get her home," I say as the girl in my arm hiccups again. "Do you know where her friends are?" I ask Nate.

He glances around. "Don't see them."

"Do you even know who she is?"

He shakes his head. "I don't think she's ever been to one of our parties before." I nod, my thoughts exactly. "You want to put her in one of the rooms upstairs?"

I shake my head and bite the inside of my mouth. I don't really want to just abandon her. Maybe she landed in my arms because fate put her there, knowing I'd help her out. Not that I'm a big believer in fate or that things happen for a reason.

"I'll take her home." I glance at Dane. "Find Jesse and come with me."

He looks like he's about to protest. Nate puts his hand on Dane's shoulder. "Go, I'll watch out for your little brother."

Dane looks at me with pleading eyes and my protest dies on my tongue. "I'm going to get her home safely, and then I'm coming back here." I deepen my voice and glare at my brother. "Stay out of trouble."

Honestly, he's a good kid. We were raised with the same morals, and I trust him. My only problem is, those working at the Scotia Gazette, the campus paper, have been out to get us. I have no idea what we did to piss them off. I only know one small mistake and my brother's name and face will be all over the front page.

He gives me a grin that's no doubt going to get him into trouble one of these days. "I'm good, bro."

I nod and hold the wiggling girl in my arms tighter. I fight through the crowd and snatch my coat up off the sofa. "Where's your coat?" I ask. Nova Scotia winters are fucking cold, and she'll freeze to death in seconds.

"I...I don't know."

"Shit." I scrub my face and sort through the pile of coats. "Any of these look familiar?"

"Nope." I put mine over her shoulders. "Wear this."

For a split second, as her gaze reaches mine, I think I see pure clarity there, and something that looks like disbelief. I angle my head, narrowing my gaze as I assess her. She stumbles a bit, and that drives home the point that she's wasted.

"Here." Pushing down my strange sense of suspicion—I'm not normally a distrustful kind of guy—I help her into my coat. Once I get her dressed, I guide her outside and the cold night air instantly chills me. I glance up and down the street, pissed that her friends would leave her like that. "Where do you live?"

"Not far. That way." She points down the sidewalk, and I hug her to me and hurry our steps, needing to get inside before I get hypothermia. I should have grabbed Dane's coat. At least she said she wasn't far. After a few blocks, as we're just about to pass by my buddy Ryan's house, where I've been staying to get away from the frat house, I turn to her again.

My breath turns to fog in front of my face when I ask, "Are we close?"

"I...don't know." She pulls away from me, and turns in a wobbly circle. Her eyes cloud over, lost and confused. I curse under my breath, and reach into the pocket of my coat, which is dangling on her body.

"Whoa," she says, flinching back as my hands connect with her waist. She blinks up at me and once again I question if she's intoxicated, until she hiccups. When did I get so para-noid? Oh, probably when the team heard the paper was out to get them.

"Just getting my keys." I nod toward Ryan's place. "My buddy Ryan lives there. He's away for the holidays and he lets me stay when I want. I need to get us both inside and warm as we figure out where you live."

"Oh, okay."

I hurry up to the house and unlock the door. She winces as I flick the lights on, and I guide her to the sofa. "Do you have a purse or anything with you?"

She glances at her waist. "I don't see one."

"Fuck."

I need to get back to the party, to my brother and his friend, but there's no way I can just leave her alone in my buddy's house. What if she gets sick, or falls asleep and wakes up confused and tries to find her way home in the cold? That has disaster written all over it.

She grips the sides of her head. "The room is spinning."

I help her up. "Yeah, I know." I walk her toward the stairs.

"Where are you taking me?" she asks.

"To bed."

LEEZA

My heart thunders against my ribs, hard enough to reverberate in my ears as Cheddar carefully guides me up the stairs and I can't help but think he can hear the pounding too. God, everything about this is wrong. I don't want to be here, trying to get dirt on this guy or any other guy on the team. I can't even believe Samantha, the chief editor at the Scotia Gazette put me up to this, threatening to replace me this semester and not give me the chief position next year when she leaves.

Sometimes it takes extreme measures to get to the truth.

That might be her philosophy, but as Cheddar pushes open a bedroom door and takes me inside, I can't say it's mine, or that I can keep my emotions out of a story. I stumble a bit, keeping up the ruse that I'm drunk. My phone is in my back pocket and Samantha has been tracking me all night, ready to run to my rescue and get pictures of Cheddar engaging in something sordid. Isn't this called entrapment?

How did I ever find myself in the middle of this?

This is not who I am, not the kind of journalism I want to do. I turn to him, about to shut this whole thing down and tell him the truth. But the warm concerned look on his face as he lightly brushes my hair back from my face, steals the words from my throat.

"This is the room I sleep in when I'm here. The sheets are freshly washed. I did laundry today." I almost snort out a laugh as I imagine the toughest guy on the hockey team home doing laundry. I actually kind of like the image...I actually kind of like him. "Why don't you crawl in. I'm going to get a glass of water, and some meds and put them on the night-stand for you, okay?" He waits for me to nod, and continues with, "I'll knock before I come back in."

My throat tightens as he gazes down at me with those gorgeous blue eyes. I don't care what Samantha said about him. Everything in my gut tells me he's a nice guy. She warned me over and over though, implying that he'd try to trick me into thinking he was a good guy because his brother was in town, and he'd be on his best behavior for the kid's sake.

Did he do something to piss off Samantha?

All I can manage to do is nod, and he walks me backward, until I'm sitting safely on the bed. "If you want to get into something more comfortable..." he says as he glances at my jeans and sweater—and not in a sexual way. He walks to his dresser, pulls out a T-shirt and a pair of sweats and brings them to me. "...you can put these on. They're big but they tie at the waist."

I take the clothes and the fresh scent of fabric softener reaches my nose. Without thinking I bring them to my face and inhale. A strange, ridiculous noise crawls out of my throat.

"Are you going to be sick?" I drop the clothes and find Cheddar squatting in front of me, concern dancing in his eyes as they assess me. "I can take you to the bathroom."

"No...I should leave."

"Nope. You're not going anywhere."

It's crazy, because I don't want to go anywhere. I want to sleep in his bed tonight, and this is all so out of character for me. "Your brother. He needs you."

He exhales and scrubs his fingers through his hair. "He and his buddy are staying in my dorm room. Nate will take care of them." He pulls his phone from his pocket, and the warmest smile comes over his face as he reads something.

"What?" I ask.

His hair falls forward with a quick shake of his head. "Nothing, just a friend."

Wait!

Is he reading our exchange from earlier tonight? If so, is that how he smiles when he reads messages from me—or rather Lisa? Yes, Samantha insisted I go on the app and friend Cheddar. I didn't want to, so she went ahead and set the whole profile up, and swiped on Rhys Taylor, which she somehow found out was Cheddar's real name. This is all so horrible.

My heart pounds so hard it hurts all the way to my throat. Honestly, I couldn't hate myself any more than I already do. I stare at the man with a player reputation. So what if he does? That doesn't mean he's a bad guy, or takes women home without consent, like Samantha assured me he did, and we just needed proof. Of course, I want to shut down guys like that, but everything in my gut—and his actions tonight—tell me he's not that guy.

"I...I should get changed."

He stands and hesitates. "Bathroom is across the hall, and I'm going to run downstairs to get you water. Can you make it by yourself or do you need help?"

"I can make it."

He nods and my gaze drops to take in his perfect backside as he walks to the door. "Wait," he says and turns back to me. He comes back to me, a look of determination in his eyes. What is he doing?

"Phone?"

"What?"

"I want to put my contact information into your phone." He jerks his thumb over his shoulder. "I'll only be across the hall, but if I don't hear you and you need me, you can call."

I swallow the guilt and hand over my phone. He puts his information in, and calls himself. "There, now I have yours." He angles his head. "It's Leeza, right?"

He knows my name?

How the hell does the hottest guy on the hockey team know my name? More importantly, why do I like that so much? I'm not into players. I'm a serious student and have my journalism career to focus on. I shake my head to clear it, working to convince myself that it's not important if he knows my name.

Wait, does he know I work for the gazette?

"Yes," I say. "It's Leeza."

"I've seen you around, but we've never met. I'm Cheddar, but I think you already know that."

"Everyone knows that," I mumble and try to remember I'm supposed to be intoxicated. "I should sleep."

"Agreed. I'll be right back." He leaves and quietly clicks the door shut. I listen to his footsteps on the stairs and I hurry out of my clothes and into his. I shoot off a text to Samantha that nothing is happening, and she can go home, and by the time I hear him coming up the stairs, I'm all tucked into his bed. He knocks.

"Are you decent?"

"Yes, come in."

My phone pings repeatedly, and he glances at me as he sets the water down. "Sounds like one of your friends might be trying to find you after all."

"I'll answer in a second." He hesitates. "Thanks for the water, and meds."

He nods and backs up. "If you need anything..."

"I'm good, thanks. Can you get the lights?"

"Sure."

"Night, Rhys."

He spins so fast, I nearly fall out of bed. "What?"

Oh God, no one calls him that. I only know that's his real name from the app we've been using.

"Peace," I say quickly and hold my hand up and spread my index and middle fingers. His eyes narrow in on me, and I hold my breath. If he figures out who I really am and what

I've been doing he's going to toss me out the window and into the cold and I don't blame him. "Peace," I say again and his shoulders relax.

"Peace," he responds. "See you in the morning."

The door clicks shut again, and as I hear the shower down the hall turn on, I grab my phone.

Samantha: What is going on?

Me: He tucked me in. He's not who you think he is.

Samantha: You don't need to stay any longer tonight.

Oh, she's worried about my safety now, is she? I'm not worried, though. Not once tonight was I worried. I see the way he acts on campus, loud, obnoxious, the life of the party. The girls love him and he loves them back. Yet...there's a different side to Rhys. A quiet, soft side that I've gotten to know through our texts. That side came out tonight when he brought me here. Maybe I'll stick with this ruse, and do an article disputing Samantha's claims. That would get me fired in a hurry. But do I really need the chief editors position next year? Yeah, I kind of do.

Me: As soon as he falls asleep, I'll leave.

. . .

Samantha: Fine, we'll meet tomorrow and come up with a new plan.

I set my phone down and snuggle back on the pillow, bringing the T-shirt to my nose to catch hints of fabric softener, and... Rhys. The guy really does have two personas, and I don't think he's playing nice on the app to get into my pants. Samantha is wrong about that. Heck, he has no idea what Lisa even looks like. Truthfully, Lisa or Leeza...neither of us are his type. Although I really do enjoy texting with him.

My phone lights up and I exhale a huff, expecting more from Samantha, but my heart jumps as a message comes through the dating app.

Rhys: Hey...still up?

I run my finger across the phone and realize how hard I'm smiling, much like the smile I saw on Rhys' face earlier, when he checked his phone. I'm about to message back when the journalist side of me kicks in. This could be a good opportunity to test his integrity.

Me: I'm up. How was your night?

Rhys: A bit strange actually.

Me: Your brother get into trouble?

. . .

Rhys: No, there was a girl on campus, and she needed some help.

I sit up a bit straighter and two things go through my mind. He knows I'm Leeza and feeling me out, or he's just an honest, open guy who's misjudged.

Me: Did you help her?

Rhys: Yeah, actually I'm at my buddy's house, and I put her to bed. She was pretty drunk and I couldn't find her friends.

Me: That was nice of you.

Don't do it, Leeza. Don't freaking do it!

Me: Was she pretty?

God, I am so pathetic.

Rhys: Yeah, she's pretty. Not as pretty as you, though.

Like a silly girl with a crush, my pulse jumps in my neck.

. . .

Me: You have no idea what I look like.

Rhys: Doesn't matter. I like...this.

I settle back into my pillow as I imagine him doing the same, liking this texting back and forth a lot too. I also like that our calls are not sexual in nature. I like asking questions about his team and he always praises the guys, telling me how they visit the hospitals and want to set good examples for the rookies. I honestly don't see the toxic culture the editor-in-chief talks about. When Rhys asks me questions, he's always respectful and curious, wanting to know about my life and my plans. I'm always careful to share what I can. I can't have him finding out what I do. Once again, another burst of guilt moves through me.

Toying with the T-shirt I'm wearing and rereading his messages, my lids close, and for the briefest of seconds I feel a tinge of disappointment that this conversation always stays clean.

What the hell, Leeza?

I push that thought down, even though there is a part of me —maybe even a huge part—that would like to know what it's like to be touched or kissed by the sweet man texting me— the sweet man in the room across the hall—not the one who showboats at parties. For the next thirty minutes, I text with a guy I can't believe I'm falling for. Not that we could ever have a relationship. If he ever found out what I was up to, he'd never want anything to do with me and I can't blame him. He stops texting and I think he's falling asleep. I know I am.

Me: Am I keeping you up?

Rhys: I could ask you the same. Oh no, wait, you're three hours earlier in Alberta.

Me: Yeah, but the holidays are killing me. I'll be glad when I get back to my regular routine.

Rhys: I'll be glad when you're back too. Tomorrow night, right?

Me: Yup.

Rhys: Are we finally going to meet?

Me: We'll see. Night, Rhys.

Rhys: Night, Lisa.

I set my phone down, my heart full of...happiness. I roll and tuck my hands under his pillow, liking that he's in the next room, watching over me. My lids drift shut and the next thing

I know, banging sounds downstairs wake me. I slide from the bed, make a quick trip to the bathroom, and quietly go down the stairs.

The second I round the corner and find Rhys, or rather Cheddar, standing before the stove, dressed in nothing but low-hanging sweats, all my girly parts go weak, but it's nothing compared to what my body does when he turns, and smiles, and points to the table where a big glass of juice awaits me.

"Sit. Bacon and eggs. It helps with the hangover."

I swallow against a tight throat. Honest to God, if this man is playing me, and really is part of the toxic culture in hockey, and I refuse to write an article on him, I risk losing the coveted position at the Gazette.

But if he isn't playing me and isn't part of the toxic culture, and I *do* write the article, then I risk losing a chance at the man I'm falling for. Either way, I'm screwed.

3

RHYS

I take my last bite of bacon and set my fork down, staring at the gorgeous girl across from me. "If you have no plans, why don't you come along?" I'm not sure why, but I'm just not ready to let her go yet. It's strange. Just chatting with her this morning, I felt like I knew her forever. She's as easy to talk to as Lisa. It's weird, I barely know either one, but I have the strangest feeling I could fall for both of them.

"I don't want to intrude. You're here with your brother and his friend."

I snort. "Trust me. Dane would rather hang out with a beautiful woman over me. He'll enjoy it. Just don't listen to any of his bullshit. He has a lot to learn about women."

Her head lifts, her interest piqued. "What do you mean?"

"He's young and stupid and thinking with his..." I glance down. "Well, you know."

She laughs. "I guess I could say I hear the same about you."

I cringe. Yeah, it's a side of me everyone knows, and you know what, she doesn't know me well and isn't looking to hook up, so maybe I can shelve that side while we tour the city with my brother and his friend. Maybe I can simply be myself around her. I feel my shoulders relaxing as that idea settles into my brain.

"You shouldn't believe everything you hear."

She lifts her phone and pulls up social media. "Should I not believe everything I see either?"

I snatch her phone away. "No. How about we just hang out and you can make up your own mind."

Her smile is sweet, and soft, and it curls around me in the oddest way. "I like…that."

I angle my head and eye her. Something in the way she worded that reminds me of Lisa, and I'm about to ask her if they know one another when my phone pings. I grab it from the table and flip it.

"I'm surprised he's up."

"Dane?"

My stomach tightens and I sit up a little straighter as I read the message. "Mother fucker."

"Uh oh."

"Uh oh is right. I need to go." I stand and reach for our empty plates. "I should never have left him."

"I'm sorry, Cheddar. It was all my fault." I turn back to see her and take in the paleness of her face.

"Hey, no. None of this is your fault." Jesus, she's really fucking upset and I hate everything about the guilt swimming in her big blue eyes. I touch her chin lightly and lift her face to mine. "Everything is okay, Leeza. I promise."

That soft easy smile, even though it's forced, nearly takes the air from my lungs. Okay, wait, maybe hanging out with her is wrong. I'm sort of trying to build a relationship with Lisa, and I don't want to string two women along. "If you want me to take you home—"

"No, I think I'd like to take you up on your offer." I swallow and her face tightens at my reaction. "If you've changed—"

"No, not at all. We just...have to pick my brother up from Nate's sister's place."

Her eyes go wide. "He did not?"

"Oh yeah. Little fucker did."

"After you warned him not to mess with her?"

I eye her as something niggles in my brain, something that questions her sobriety last night. "You remember that?'"

She twists the hem of my T-shirt between her fingers like she's said something she shouldn't have. "Yeah, parts."

"Do you want to shower here and wear something of mine, or do you want me to take you back to your place?" I have no idea why she's paling again. It's a simple question.

"Here," she says fast, like the idea of me taking her to her place is out of the question. Maybe she has house rules about guys or something.

"Go on up, then. Grab some clean clothes out of the dresser. I stay here enough that I keep a lot of things here and you'll find a spare toothbrush in the bottom of the bathroom cabinet."

She nods and I stare after her, liking what I'm looking at as she disappears upstairs, but I don't have time for admiration, not when my brother might have made a big fucking mistake.

I hurry to load the dishwasher, turn it on and dash upstairs. I go to my bedroom, grab some clothes from my drawer and when I turn to go into Ryan's room to dress, I find Leeza standing in the doorway dressed in nothing but a big fluffy towel, that has me tenting my sweats. I let my hands fall, using my clean clothes to cover myself.

"I...uh...I was just getting my clothes," I explain. She stands in the doorway, like her legs aren't quite working. Maybe she's too afraid to come in when I'm in there, now that she's sober. "I'll just get out of your way." I take a step toward her.

"It's your room. You can change here."

I gulp as my feet come to a resounding halt. "Oh, you want to go to Ryan's room to change?"

"No. I wasn't suggesting that."

Holy shit, what is she suggesting?

"I'm not going to kick you out of your own room again. You left last night because of me." She circles her finger. "You turn that way, and I'll turn this way." She walks to my bed, to where her clothes are laid out, and turns her back to me. Does she not realize I can see her in the mirror? Maybe she does and goddammit, maybe she wants me to look.

Fuck me twice.

I turn to avoid temptation, and since I showered last night, and don't have time for another this morning, I quickly dress, and when she's done, I turn and take in my sweats on her. She's in the same sweater she wore last night.

A few minutes later we're outside and sliding into my car, which has been sitting in Ryan's driveway. I vaguely remember where Kendra lives. I pull into the driveway and the front door opens, and out walks my asshole brother, looking mussed and well fucked.

I'm going to kill him.

I crook my finger and at least he looks a bit worried. He should be. I'm going to kick his ass. I'm about to open my door and grab him by the scruff of the neck, stopping when Leeza's hand lands on my lap. It does two things at the same time: heat me up and cool me down. I turn to her.

"Don't be too hard on him."

If only she wasn't being too hard on me.

"Leeza—"

"They're both young, doing what young people do. You can't help who you like, or that her brother is the captain of the hockey team. Also, is it fair, Cheddar? Shouldn't she do what is right for her, what's in her heart? She's old enough to make her own decisions and shouldn't be a puppet on a string, manipulated by some marionette."

Why do I get the sense she's talking about something personal here?

"Her brother just worries about her."

"I understand. You worry about your brother too. But I'm guessing it was all consensual..." I scrub my face as Dane opens the back door. "Last night, you took me home and cared for me, showing your brother how it's supposed to be done. I think you both come from a good place."

I smile at that. She's pretty astute for a girl I just met. "What did I tell you?" I growl at my kid brother as he slides into the car.

"Sorry, bro."

"Sorry, bro. That's all you have to say?" Leeza eyes me, but I have to be hard on the kid. I don't want him getting his ass kicked in the streets, or booted from the team next year.

"I like her, and I think she likes me too."

"Clearly." I adjust the rearview mirror and catch his grin. He might like her now, but it will be eight months before he's going here full time and I'm sure they'll forget all about each other. I relax and let my worries go. "Dane, this is Leeza. Do you remember her from last night?

"Yeah." Dane leans forward and grabs the back of Leeza seat. "How are you feeling?" I smile at his concern.

Leeza folds her hand on her lap and stretches them out. "Great. I slept it off, and your brother took good care of me."

"Did he cook you breakfast?"

"Of course. Did you cook Kendra breakfast?" she asks with a raised brow.

"No, I left her sleeping, and didn't want to mess around in her kitchen, but do you think we could grab a breakfast sandwich and coffee so I can bring something back to her for when she wakes up?

I nod, my heart warming at his consideration. Maybe he'll do okay here after all, and maybe he was just showing off in front of his friend last night, pretending to be something he wasn't —something everyone expects of him—especially since he's my kid brother. Shit, maybe I'm not setting a good example at all. But today, I plan to be Rhys, not Cheddar, and show him it's okay to be who you really are. If people don't like Rhys, screw them. I laugh to myself. It took me long enough to figure that shit out.

"Yeah sure, kid." I back out of the driveway. "Where's Jesse?"

"Asleep in your dorm."

"Alone, I hope?"

He holds his hands up. "What Jesse does is not my business."

"He's in my room, which makes it my business. Let's go get breakfast, deliver it, and go get him. You still want to see the campus and sights today, don't you?"

He nods. "Will you be joining us, Leeza?"

She glances at him over her shoulder. "If that's okay with you?"

"It is, as long as you're up for it, and you're not too hung over."

She nods emphatically and I don't know about her, but whenever I was that wasted, I was hurting the next day. I guess the water, meds and breakfast helped her recover faster.

The streets are pretty quiet this morning, so I make through the drive-thru fast, grab the food, and deliver it back to Kendra. Dane takes so long inside I wonder if he went back to bed with her. I'm just about to go get him when he comes outside a big smile on his face.

"Get in," I grumble. As soon as he's buckled, I go back to the dorm and park. "Come inside and stay warm," I say to Leeza. "I'll get Jesse." I hurry upstairs and find him alone in my bed, and for that I'm happy. Although by the mussed sheets, I'm not sure he was alone all night.

I nudge him. "Rise and shine, Jesse." He grumbles and I wave the breakfast sandwich in front of his nose. Like any young, growing guy, he rises up and rubs his stomach. "Get dressed and meet us downstairs." I drop the bag on the nightstand, and head back downstairs to find Dane and Leeza sitting close and talking and a weird, sharp pang of jealousy hits me in the chest.

Whoa, what the hell?

"Back off," I blurt out before I can stop myself, and Dane's head lifts. He grins, a knowing little grin I'd like to smack off his face. Honestly, I shouldn't be possessive of Leeza. I barely know her. Despite that, I feel like I do. I have this strange draw to her, a strange sense of familiarity.

Jesse comes barreling down the stairs, his clothes and hair disheveled. "Dude," he says to Dane and pats him on the back. "What a night, eh?"

Since I don't want to hear the details and I'm sure Leeza doesn't either, I pipe up. "How about we walk the campus and then hit up the boardwalk and find a place for lunch?"

"Um, actually I have plans for lunch," Dane announces a sheepish grin on his face.

Jesse pulls out the breakfast sandwich, bites into it and adds, "Yeah, me too."

I shake my head. "I thought you guys wanted to experience the city."

Dane nudges Jesse. "We are."

"Dane," I warn. "I told you—"

He throws his hands out, all innocent. "What? We're going skating at the oval. I heard a few people at the party putting a plan together last night."

I narrow my eyes. "You're going in a group?"

"Yup."

I nod. I guess that's okay. Better than one on one time with Kendra. Next year I'll be out of here, unable to look out for him. Right now, I can only guide him into making smart choices.

I glance at Leeza, and I'm about to speak when my phone pings. I pull it from my pocket and check it to find a message from one of my buddies. It's nothing urgent so I tuck my phone away and ask Leeza, "Feel like skating later?"

"I'm not keeping you from something, or someone, am I?"

I get it. I have a reputation, so she expects that I'll be hooking up over the holidays. "I cleared the day to spend with these two." I glance outside and shove my hands into my pockets and decide to tell her what I really think. "I'd love it if you came."

A smile lights up her face, and as I take her in, I try not to remember her standing in my room with nothing on but a towel. "I think it will be fun."

"Okay, let's show these guys around." She turns and walks toward the door and as my gaze takes her in, my body reacts. Goddammit, there are a lot of things I'd like to show her too, and every one of them involves us being naked. But I'm so over fast hook-ups. I want something more permanent, which is why I went on the app. I want to get to know a girl, have her get to know me as Rhys, not Cheddar.

Wait, did she call me Rhys last night?

LEEZA

I wobble in my skates and grab Rhys' arm before I face plant. "I'm not very good at this."

"You're doing just fine," he lies, and I laugh.

"I'm making a fool of myself."

"No, you're not."

"You're right. No one is looking at me when I'm with you."

He angles his head, his brow furrowed together as he adjusts his hat. "What's that supposed to mean?"

I laugh and wave my hand, catching the way the women are admiring him and looking at me with envy. No one has ever looked at me with envy before, and while I don't exactly revel in that, I do love the intent way Rhys looks at me, especially when he doesn't think I'm watching.

"You're like a God around this place, loved by everyone," I inform him, even though I'm not telling him something he doesn't already know.

An almost sad look comes over his face, and it wraps around my heart. "I'm just me, Leeza."

This is Rhys I'm talking to, the sweet guy from the app, not the life of the party Cheddar everyone knows and I strangely find myself falling a little more for him. Why does he keep this side of himself hidden? I'm not sure, but since last night, since taking me home, he's been gifting me with insight into the man beneath the jersey, and I don't think he's putting on a false show for his little brother. I think this is the real Rhys, and I like him a lot.

Maybe that's why I absurdly told him not to leave the room while we changed. Holy hell, what was I thinking? That's so unlike me. I think though, there's a part of me that really likes his attention, and maybe, just maybe wants to know what it feels like to be touched, kissed by him—to be the sole focus of his desire.

A fine shiver goes through me and he tugs me to him and I almost moan as his big body dwarfs mine, making me feel warm and safe. "Are you cold?"

"Maybe a little," I fib. Wait, why am I fibbing? Maybe I should just come right out and tell him what he does to me. There's no denying that I want him, and I think he might like me too. Oh right, I know why I can't do that.

I'm getting close to him to do a story on him.

Ugh, kill me now.

He narrows his eyes. "Hey, are you okay?"

I swallow and try to put on a happy face, as his brother, Jesse and a group of girls all skate by and wave to us. "Yeah, I am."

"I think you disappeared for a second there. Something on your mind?"

Oh, if he only knew.

I gesture toward the small kiosk serving up drinks and snacks. "Yeah, I was thinking a hot chocolate would be nice."

He laughs. "Let's do it."

His palm leaves the small of my back and captures my hand and as we skate toward the kiosk, Samantha glides by, her gaze going from me to Rhys, back to me again. Rhys scrubs his face, and averts his gaze.

"Do you two know each other?" I ask, taking in his strange behavior and the snarl on Sam's face when she looked at him.

"Something like that."

My stomach instantly tightens and I have a suspicious feeling they might have hooked up in the past. All I know is there's bad blood there, and maybe that's why Samantha is out to get him. I want to ask, but don't want to make him suspicious.

My mind races with questions as he starts skating, and I try not to look like such a novice next to him as we head to the back of the line forming at the kiosk. He lets my hand go and just like that, my stupid skates go out from underneath me and I'm flat out on my back, my head hitting the ice a little too hard.

"Leeza." Rhys' voice reverberates in my brain as he drops to his knees and brings me to his body, cradling me in his arms. "Are you okay?"

I blink as he carefully examines my eyes. "I don't even know what happened."

"This was a bad idea."

I touch his face. "No, I liked coming here with you." His face softens but concern still brims in his eyes. "It's just been a long time since I've been on skates."

"Let me take you home."

Panic erupts inside me. We can't go to my place. I can't risk him finding out that Leeza and Lisa are one in the same. My heart thumps. I hate betraying him like this, but I guess at the end of the day, I'm glad Samantha put me on the case, because I'm not going to fabricate a story for shock value. That's not why I want to be a journalist.

"If your friend's place is still empty, maybe we can go there." His brow furrows in confusion, and I jerk my thumb out. "It's closer and maybe the faster I lie down the better."

"Good plan."

His brother comes to a halt beside us. "Leeza, are you okay?"

I nod and Rhys explains that he's taking me back to Ryan's and that he'll check in with him and Jesse later.

"Yeah, we're good," Dane assures Rhys. He zeroes in on me. "I'm sorry you're hurt, Leeza. If you need anything—"

"She's got me," Rhys says, his voice so possessive and commanding, his brother backs up an inch, a grin on his face.

"Yeah, she does," Dane adds with a nod, and then the two exchange a look I don't understand. Before I can ask what's going on, Rhys pulls me to my feet and scoops me up. I glance around a little embarrassed as a crowd stares on.

"I can walk," I say quietly.

"And I can carry you." He takes me to a bench, keeping a close eye on me as he unties my skates and then his. Since I rented mine, he drops them off and takes me to his car, setting me inside.

"We could have walked, it's not far."

"You banged your head pretty hard. Maybe we should go to the hospital."

I touch the back of my head. "Not even a bump," I tell him. "Good thing I was wearing a thick hat." I take his hand and put it on the back of my head and he feels around, the rough pads of his thumbs lightly feeling their way around and the sensations rocket through my body and settle between my legs. I swallow and his hand goes still. I turn his way and I'm pretty damn sure he knows what his touch is doing to me.

Five minutes later, he's carrying me inside his friend's place. We take off our boots and coats at the front door, and he's taking me up to his bed, which I neatly made after sleeping in it last night. My phone pings, and I'm sure it's Samantha, so I ignore it.

"Do you need to get that?" I shake my head no, as he pulls his phone out and frowns as he checks it. Is he waiting for a message from Lisa? My throat clogs with guilt, and a part of me is tempted to just blurt out the truth. I just...don't want to hurt him or for him to hate me.

I glance at my phone and read the message from Samantha.

Samantha: You're supposed to be the one playing the player, not the other way around. Don't fall for it, you're just another notch, you'll see and if you don't get me my article you can forget about becoming editor-in-chief.

. . .

I get it, she thinks he's the one playing me, but as he pulls the covers down, I don't think either of us are playing any kind of game here and I can't even seem to think about the job, not when my body is burning from the inside out.

I turn my phone over on the nightstand so he can't see it, and slide between the sheets. As he tucks me in, something comes over me and before I can stop myself, I slide my hands around his neck, my pulse pounding so hard in my throat, I can barely breathe. Am I really doing this?

"I...don't think I'm supposed to be left alone. You know, possible concussion."

His eyes narrow in on mine, a careful assessment that sets my blood on fire. "I thought—"

Sexual tension arcs between us and his chest rises and falls a bit faster. "It doesn't hurt to be careful."

Which makes me wonder why I'm not being careful—I should be making decisions with my head, not my body and heart. I shouldn't be doing this, I shouldn't be pulling his lips to mine, but I can't seem to stop. The only thing I can do is blame my behavior on a brain injury. Maybe I hit my head harder than I thought, or maybe I simply, just once, want to be coveted and touched by this sweet man hovering over me in his bed—a sweet man he keeps hidden but has exposed to me numerous times.

Seconds before his lips touch mine, he stiffens, like he's having second thoughts, and I go completely still. "Cheddar?" I say about to scramble away. Oh God, maybe I've read this all wrong.

"Leeza," he says quickly and puts his hand on my arm to stop me. "You banged your head. I just want to make sure this is what you want. That you're making decisions you'd make if you hadn't fallen."

As he stares down at me, checking in on me and looking for consent, I fall a little more for him. Sam is so wrong about him. "I want you," I say quietly, and put my hands around his head again.

"I want you too." He glances at the nightstand where we set our phones. "I just...I should probably take care of—"

"Me," I say, and lift until his lips are on mine, and the second I feel the softness of his mouth, a moan catches in my throat and whatever it was he wanted to do is long gone from his brain, because he's kissing me with heat and hunger, a growl rumbling in the depths of his throat.

I inch up, lift my arms and he peels my sweater off, his gaze turning feral as he takes in my lacy bra. With deft hands, he unhooks my bra and I don't want to spend too much time thinking how easy that was for him. A second later, he's standing, and I can't tear my gaze away as he peels off his sweater, unzips his jeans, and kicks them away.

Holy freaking God.

My gaze bumps up and down over his hard abs, coming to rest on his steel cock. My breathing changes, becomes fast as he climbs back on the bed, moves between my legs and releases the knot holding his big sweatpants to my hips. But I'm not the only one breathing hard, or shaking. I'm not sure if he's like this with every girl—and in this moment, I don't want to think about it—but for a man with his reputation, he seems a little off kilter at the moment.

He removes my pants, and spreads my legs, his gaze going from my face, to my breasts to my sex. He takes a couple fast breaths, and his head lifts, gaze locked on mine. "You are so damn beautiful, Leeza."

I gulp at the hunger in his eyes—the honesty and vulnerability in his tone—and as he devours me with his gaze, I can't say that any man has ever looked at me the way he's looking at me right now. He bends forward and buries his face between my legs and as he licks me, his thumb going to my clit, my entire body trembles and my hips come off the bed.

"Yes," I say. "Ohmigod, yes." I run my fingers through is hair, holding him to me as pleasure spikes in my body. He licks and laps and sucks and nibbles and never in my life has oral sex been so mind-blowing. Before I even realize what's happening, I begin to burn from the inside out and he must know what's going on with me, because he applies more pressure to my clit, and inserts a finger and the second he does, my body breaks around him.

"Rhys," I cry out, my delirious, lust-saturated brain shutting down, as pleasure pulses through me, and I soak his face with my liquid release. I pant and struggle to breathe as he stays between my legs, letting me ride out the orgasm, but as soon as I do, he expertly begins to arouse me up again.

What is this man doing to me?

He climbs up my body, pressing hot wet kisses to my trembling flesh before his lips crash down on mine, eating at my mouth with the hunger of a starved animal who'd just taken down its prey. No man has ever quite wanted me like this, and I have to say, it excites and thrills me, and fills me with a new kind of confidence. I wrap my legs around him and he growls, and reaches into the nightstand. He produces a condom and bites into the wrapper, tearing it open. Once again, his eyes seek mine out, seeking permission, and I nod quickly.

He slides the condom on with expertise and falls over me again. His hard cock presses against my sex, and I wiggle, trying to force him in. While he seems as anxious as I do, he slows things down and shifts lower, like he wants to draw tonight out, because it could be our one and only time and that thought brings tightness to my heart. My thoughts scatter as he takes one nipple into his mouth and I roll my head from side to side, taking pleasure in the delicious way his hot tongue laves and savors my hard bud.

I rake my hands through his hair and move against him, eager for everything. "That is so good," I murmur and my words seem to do something to him. He angles his body, taking his cock into his hand and I go up on my elbows, wanting to watch him slide inside me.

My breath is coming so fast, I'm getting lightheaded, and I bend my knees, and let them fall open. He growls, and the sound of pure need curls around me, driving my desire.

"You want this, Leeza? You want my cock?" I nod, not sure I can actually vocalize anything. "That's good, because I want to be inside your gorgeous pussy." He lightly pets my sex, and a second later, he's over my body, his mouth claiming mine as he powers his hips forward and pushes all the way inside me, filling me like I've never been filled before. I try to gasp, to groan, to claw at the bed, but he swallows my sound and pins my hands above my head, taking full control of me and I love it.

He inches out, and the friction creates heat and pleasure. Once again, my brain shuts down, nothing existing but this man and the sheer pleasure he's giving me. I lift my hips as he powers back in, encouraging him to give me everything he has and then some. Soon enough, we're moving in sync, creating a rhythm of lovers, each giving and taking and somehow knowing exactly what the other needs.

My body quakes and small ripples begin in my core. "Fuck yeah," he murmurs and lets go of my hands. I slide them around his back as he buries his face in the crook of my neck. I want to hang on, want this to last forever, but my body gives in and my sex pulses around his steel cock.

"Leeza," he murmurs, and drives into me, going still as my sex milks his release. He grunts, and trembles, moisture breaking out on his flesh as he too gives himself over to the pleasure.

I hold him to me, letting each pulse of his cock reverberate through my body and loving every second of it. He lifts his head and the second his gaze lands on mine, my heart misses a beat, the intimacy in what we just shared creating a new closeness between us. I'm sure he feels it every bit as much as I do.

"Hey," he says quietly, and lightly brushes his lips over mine. "You okay?"

"I'm better than okay?"

He shakes his head, like he's trying to get it on right, and I totally understand that. "Next time, I'll try to go slower." His grin is soft and sheepish and wraps around me like a warm blanket.

I arch a brow. "There's going to be a next time?"

He laughs and brushes my hair back. "Of course. Wait, you want there to be a next time, don't you?"

"Yes," I answer honestly. How can there be, though? When he finds out who I am and why I sought him out at the party—and on the app—I'm sure he'll never speak to me again.

He exhales and his eyes are warm, brimming with apology. "I just...this time, I really wanted you, and I kind of lost it. I'm sorry, babe. I'll do better next time."

"Nothing to be sorry about." I brush my hands through his hair. He isn't the only one who lost it. His warm, tender gaze locks on mine, and my heart pinches tight. Oh God, I need to tell him everything, but how, and if I do, would my actions be a deal breaker for him? I can't say as I'd blame him, really.

"Hey, are you sure you're okay?" He lightly brushes the back of his knuckles over my cheek.

"Yes," I croak out, even though I'm not and he's astute enough to sense it.

"Thirsty?" he asks as I swallow. Hard.

Needing a moment of reprieve, I nod, and he stands, and tucks me in. "I'll be right back." He tugs on the sweats I was wearing and snatches his phone off the nightstand. I watch him go, and while my body should be relaxed after sex it's not. I'm completely wound up. I reach for my phone, and notice I have a message in the dating app. I open it and my pulse leaps in my throat as I read the message from Rhys.

Rhys: Can I see you tonight?

The room instantly spins around me, as everything Samantha said about him bounces around inside my brain. Maybe he is playing me, and maybe I should write the article on the toxic culture in hockey, using him as an example. Yeah, sure I'll get the editor-in-chief position and secure my future, but if I do write it and I'm wrong, I risk losing Rhys and the future I might actually want more.

So, what are you going to do, Leeza?

I walk around Storm House, the New Year's Eve party in full swing. I walk by a room where my brother and Jesse and a few others are playing a drinking game. Kendra is nowhere to be found, and I think that's a good thing.

You know who else is nowhere to be found? Leeza, or Lisa. Unease erupts in my stomach. After sex this morning, Leeza said she had things to take care of and practically bolted out the front door. As she fled, I asked her if she'd be here tonight, and she said she would be, but she had a paper to write first.

We're on Christmas break, so I have no idea what paper she has to write...unless. Bile punches into my throat as I glance around and spot Samantha. What the hell is she doing here? She hates hockey and parties, and me in particular.

I pull my phone from my pocket and check my app. As suspicion wells up inside of me, I shoot off another message to Lisa, asking her when she's going to be here. I stare at the phone, waiting for a response, but none comes. I tuck my phone away as Samantha seeks me out.

"Samantha," I say, bracing myself, because she looks like she wants to murder me. It's been years since we hooked up, and she's hated me ever since. "Happy New Year."

She laughs, but it's humorless. "Oh, it will be. For me anyway."

"What's that supposed to mean?"

Her grin is sly and she has a look of victory on her face. "You'll see."

I take a sip of beer, and it's flat on my tongue. "Did you come here tonight to play cryptic games with me?"

She points an accusing finger. "I'm not the one who plays games, Cheddar."

"I don't know what I ever did to hurt you, but I'm sorry," I say and truly mean it.

"You're sorry," she shoots back. "Sorry for sleeping with me and then acting like you didn't know me."

I lower my head, my stomach cramping. "I'm not that guy anymore, Sam. I never meant to hurt you. I thought it was just a hook-up."

"Maybe you should have clarified that with me first to let me know where I stood before you took me back to my place."

"You're right, I should have." I honestly had no idea that she wanted more from me. I was just a guy who partied. Everyone wanted a nibble of Cheddar and no one took me seriously. At least, I didn't think they did. Leeza though, I thought she saw me for me, but now...I think things aren't quite as they seem.

She folds her arms and gives me a look that suggests she doesn't believe me. "You're only putting on a show because your brother is here. I know who you really are..." She nods and gestures to the front door, to where Leeza is standing. "So does she." Sam laughs. "Looks like the player has been played."

"Leeza," I say my heart squeezing tight when I spot her standing in the doorway, nervously nibbling on her lower lip, a sheet of paper in her hand. "What..." I swallow, hard. "What have you done?"

I honestly don't need to ask, because I already know. All this time, she's been playing me. That first night I brought her back to Ryan's place, when I silently questioned her sobriety, she called me Rhys. I was sure of it, even though she tried to play it off. Then this morning, during sex, she called me Rhys again. There's no way she could have known my real name, unless...

"Hi Lisa," I say, as all the pieces fall into place.

"Cheddar..." She shakes her head and corrects herself. "Rhys. I'm...I'm..."

Samantha squares her shoulders. "Let the show begin." She walks over to Leeza and takes the paper.

I shake my head and start to walk away. "Rhys, please..." Leeza reaches for me, and I jerk my arm away. "It's not what you think."

"Are you telling me you weren't pretending to be drunk to see if I would try to take advantage of you?" She pales. "That you weren't pretending to be Lisa on an app, looking to get dirt on me?"

"I fell for you," she blurts out. "I fell for Rhys Taylor."

"You don't know who Rhys Taylor is Leeza, or is it Lisa?"

"I do know," she says, a new kind of panic in her voice. "We spent hours talking, and I loved every minute of it. During those conversations, you showed me with words who you really were, and when you took care of me the other night, and we went skating, and I fell and you took me to your bedroom, and well...you know. You showed me with actions who you really were."

"Who am I, Leeza?"

She blinks rapidly, a pleading look in her eyes as she says, "You're the nicest, sweetest guy I know."

I snort out a laugh. "And this is how you repay me?"

Her hair flares as she shakes her head hard. "It's not what you think."

"Does it matter?" I rake my fingers through my hair, my heart aching in my chest. "I thought we could have something great together."

"But you wanted to see Lisa."

"Yeah, to tell her about you, and that I was falling for you. I wanted to be a stand-up guy and do it face to face. What does any of this matter now? I don't even know who you are, and now you probably destroyed our team's reputation, painting them all with the same cruel brush you painted me. Fine, if you wanted to take me down, then take me down. None of the guys deserved it." I turn my back to her.

"You don't deserve it either."

I spin back around. "What?"

I stare at Leeza as Sam clears her throat. "Okay everyone, listen up." A crowd gathers as Sam raises her voice and starts reading the article, and my heart lodges somewhere in my throat. I knew the paper was out to get dirt on the team, but how could Leeza have done this? How could she have tricked me, even going so far as to sleep with me? I thought she wanted me...wanted us.

"Wait, what did you just say?" I ask Samantha, as her face turns a dark shade of red. Anger flares in her eyes as she crinkles the paper in her hand and glares at Leeza.

"What is this shit?"

"I told the truth," Leeza says. "The guys on the team might sleep around, but what business is that of ours or anyone else's? They're grown men, and they're not hurting anyone, and as far as I can see, every hook-up is consensual, just like ours was. He's a good leader on and off his team and is leaving behind a good healthy culture for the rookies." She catches Dane's eye, and he nods and smiles.

"This is ridiculous," Samantha practically shouts. I'm pretty sure steam is going to come out of Sam's ears as she takes a step toward Leeza. "You know you're fired, right?"

"I know." Leeza lifts her chin. "I'm not going to falsify a story because you wanted revenge. If that's the kind of journalism the Gazette expects from me, I don't want any part of it. I'll find work elsewhere."

Everything inside me softens as Samantha storms out of Storm House. "Nothing to see here," I say to the crowd, waving them off. As soon as they disperse, I close the distance between Leeza and me and take her hand in mine.

"Thank you."

"I'm sorry, Rhys. I didn't want to do the article. Samantha held the chief's position over my head."

"You really needed it, huh?"

"Yeah, kind of, but I'll figure out something else."

"You don't have to."

"What do you mean?"

"My aunt works at the Chronicle, here in the city. I'll make some calls."

Her eyes go wide. "I can't believe you'd do that for me, after…"

I hold my hand out. "Hi, my name is Rhys Taylor, a hockey player who's been drafted by the Boston Bulls. Want to grab a drink and get to know each other better, maybe even a kiss when the ball drops?"

Her laugh is light and joyous as she takes my hand. "Hi, I'm Leeza Hansen. I'm a budding journalist with morals and I'd love to grab that drink."

I put my arm around her and she smiles up at me.

"Rhys, I want you to know the girl you chatted with on the app, the words I spoke, that was the real me." She glances at the crinkled paper on the floor. "The words in my article, that's me too. If you give me a chance, I'd like to show you through actions who I really am, too."

"I think I'd love that," I say, and cup her chin, lifting her lips to mine.

Seconds before our lips touch, she speaks. "You know what I think I'd like?"

"What?"

Her grin is playful, sexy downright naughty and I'm not sure what she's about to tell me, I only know I'm going to like it.

"A little bit of cheddar," she answers.

I laugh and scoop her up, taking her up the stairs to my dorm room. "Forget that, you're getting a whole lot of cheddar."

FAKE OUT

Cathryn Fox

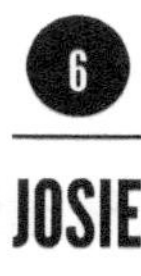

JOSIE

I stand outside on my steps and take a couple of deep, fast breaths, but the late night, cool September air does nothing to cool the anxiety racing through my veins. Is this really happening? Is Scotia Storm's center, Jesse Campbell, really coming to my place to hang out?

Technically, we're not hanging out at my place. No, we're sort of in hiding. Wait, that's not entirely true. Jesse and I aren't in hiding. We can be seen out together any time we want. It's just not something he's ever wanted—until now.

It's my best friend and roommate Kendra who is having a secret relationship with Jesse's best friend Dane. Those two are behind this 'date' between Jesse and me. Although I'm not sure I can really call it a date. I honestly don't know what to call what we're doing. I go to his games all the time, but he's never noticed me before and I'm definitely not the kind of girl he gravitates toward.

A hand lands on my arm and I turn to Kendra. "Josie, you're wearing a hole in the steps, and they're cement. Relax."

"Relax?" I practically shriek. "I'm about to hang out with Jesse Freaking Campbell."

"I don't think that's his middle name," she teases.

"Yeah, well...I'm a mess. I want to make a good first impression and..." My words fall off—probably because I just swallowed my tongue—as two big male figures move along the sidewalk toward us. "Ohmigod," I whisper under my breath.

Jesse smiles as he steps up to me, and I stare, a little star struck. I've seen him up close before, of course. I've just never been the sole focus of his attention, and holy hell, it's throwing me off my game. Not that I have game—or much experience with the opposite sex—but you get it.

Pull yourself together, Josie.

As a nursing student, I'm used to working under pressure, so I call on my skills and try to sound and appear somewhat casual as I smile back. Dane does the introductions, and my gaze drops to Jesse's lips as he says, "Hi."

Dane leans in and kisses Kendra, a risky move, considering their relationship is a secret, but it's easy to see they're having a hard time keeping their hands off one another.

"You guys ready to go?" I ask, and Kendra and Dane start down the sidewalk, leaving me with Jesse.

"Great game tonight," I say. That's a girl, keeping the conversation all about him will make chatting easier, and hey, everyone likes talking about themselves, right? Everyone but me, that is.

He gifts me with a smile. "Thanks for coming and supporting us."

"I love the game." I glance at his perfect face and admire all the hard angles. *Okay girl, stop staring before you get caught.* "You and Dane grew up together in Bass River?"

"Yup, my family owns a cattle ranch. Dane says you're a nursing student. Did you grow up here?"

Shoot, I hate when the conversation turns to me. By nature, I'm quiet and a nurturer, but sometimes people mistake me for a spoiled little rich girl when they find out I grew up on the south shore, in a very expensive area, and both my parents, as well as my grandfather, are well known surgeons. I certainly don't think of myself as a poor little anything.

Neglected child of busy parents might be a better way to describe my upbringing. But I'm out on a 'date' with Jesse and don't want to think about how my parents can't understand why I'd settle for nursing—a supporting role as they put it—when I could be a surgeon. In their eyes, it's second best, a sidekick position. That's me, second best. A girl who's never been number one to anyone.

His body brushes mine, and that's when I get a whiff of his freshly scented skin. All thoughts of my family leave my brain, and a crazy squeaking noise crawls out of my throat.

"Cold?" he asks.

"Yeah, a bit." I tighten my arms around my body to hide what I'm feeling.

"Want my jacket? I always run hot after a game."

The man runs hot even before a game. "No, that's okay. We're close."

"Where are we going anyway?" he asks, and glances around the waterfront. It's busy tonight, like it always is when everyone on campus goes out to celebrate a win.

"Didn't Dane tell you?" I ask.

"No, he said Kendra didn't tell him."

"I didn't realize it was a surprise," I say.

He nudges me and his touch sends a little thrill through me. Good God, I am so ridiculous. "Aw, come on. You don't have to keep it from me. I won't tell." He crosses his heart and offers me an adorable smile. "Scout's honor."

I laugh at that, some of the tension draining from my body. "Well, if it's Scout's honor," I tease back and point as we approach a leisure boat docked on the Halifax waterfront. "We're going for a ride on my grandfather's boat."

His jaw falls open. "No way."

"Yeah, do you like boating?"

"Who doesn't?" He frowns. "Wait, who's driving it? Is your grandfather on board?"

"No, I'm taking us out," I tell him and feel a measure of pride as he angles his head, makes a fist, and lightly taps my chin.

"Nice, Carver, nice."

I laugh at the use of my last name. "So should I call you Campbell, or soup?" Wow, look at me being all cute and witty.

He groans and throws his arms out. "The team couldn't have come up with a better nickname than soup?"

I shrug. "They had no choice. You're cursed with the name Campbell."

"Truth." He turns his attention back to the boat. "Will you teach me how to drive it?"

"Sure."

Surprise moves over his face. "Yeah?"

"Sure, why not?" We step up to the security gate and I slip my key into the padlock to open it. I catch the way Jesse is admiring the big boat as we make our way down the metal walkway, Kendra and Dane somewhere behind us.

"It looks kind of expensive. Maybe I shouldn't get behind the wheel."

"Are you planning on crashing it?" I tease.

He laughs. "No, and hey, if you're going to teach me to drive it, I can teach you something in return."

I nearly topple off the wobbling walkway. Is he talking about...sex? Does he know I'm practically a virgin? Not that there's such a thing. A broken hymen is a broken hymen but in my senior year of high school Declan was in and out so fast, I wasn't even sure we did the deed.

"Like what?" I ask hoping my voice isn't as shaky as my knees.

"If you ever make your way to our farm, I can teach you to ride a tractor." He grins and nudges me, and I swear to God if he keeps touching me, I'm going to spontaneously combust. "You never know when that skill is going to come in handy."

We step inside the boat, Kendra and Dane still making their way down the walkway, and I head to the steering wheel as Jesse whistles. "What a boat."

I glance at him over my shoulder and hope he's not thinking I'm a pampered princess. "Thanks. Come check out the wheel."

I'm about to step back and let him put his hands on the big wheel when he moves in behind me, his big hard body pressing against mine. His hips jut forward as the boat rocks, and his groin presses into my back. OMG, is that what he's working with?—and he's not even hard. If I hadn't already swallowed my tongue, I would have swallowed it again.

His big hands grip the steering wheel, stroking up and down in a manner that has my body warming and thinking very inappropriate thoughts.

"Are we taking it out?" he asks, his mouth near my ear. The heat of his breath makes thinking impossible which is probably why I'm standing here wondering exactly what it is he wants to take out. "The boat, are we taking it out?"

"Yeah, sure," I somehow manage to say. "Come outside with me, and I'l; show you how to release the lines and secure the boat fenders."

He salutes me. "Yes, ma'am."

I laugh at his antics as Kendra and Dane come onboard. "You have to do everything I say, otherwise, these two could be drifting out to sea while we remain on the dock."

"Wow, smart, bossy and take charge." He gives me a teasing grin. "Where have you been all my life?"

"Do not let us drift out to sea," Kendra warns as we step back outside and onto the wharf.

"I'm yours to teach," he says to me.

I point to the lines. "Safety first. You never step into a loop, okay? When you untie the rope, wrap it around your arm and between your thumb and finger."

"Learned that in boy scouts."

"Okay, you stay right here and do this one." I point. "I'll be right there."

"Got it." I watch him for a second, not because I'm worried he'll do it wrong but because he's simply nice to look at. Before it begins to look obvious that I'm staring, I go to work on the other rope.

A minute passes and I hear, "Oh, shit."

I glance up, and lose my balance as the rocking boat pulls on the rope, and drags me with it.

"Jesse," I yelp, and he drops what he's doing and rushes to me. I windmill my arms, and he grabs for me, only to lose his balance and splash into the water right on top of me.

I always thought I'd die if I ever found myself beneath Jesse's hard body, but I never saw it going down like this and if I don't get out from underneath him, I really am going to die. I maneuver my body until I'm free, and we both surface, gasping for breath.

"Are you okay?" he asks quickly.

No, I'm not okay. In fact, I don't think I'll ever be okay again. I just finished warning him about safety only to make a stupid mistake myself, and now here we are in the harbor.

Way to make a good first impression, Josie.

"I'm okay, are you?" I squeak out.

"This water is fucking freezing."

I sputter as the icy water from the Halifax harbour seeps into my clothes and saturates my bones. Is this what cryogenics is like? My teeth clang together. "It's colder than freezing."

With his most excellent upper body strength, Jesse easily lifts himself onto the wharf. "I got you." He reaches down, and fishes me out, effortlessly rescuing a popsicle formerly known as Josie from the icy water. My body collides with his, and I shiver hard, fearful my bones are going to shatter. "We need to get out of these clothes fast."

Oh, God are we going to get naked? We hurry onto the boat and close the door of the cabin, our friends nowhere to be found. A noise sounds from the bedroom I usually sleep in when onboard, and my gaze jerks to Jesse as heat infuses my body—pushing back the cold.

"Naked, now," Jesse orders as I shiver, my brain too frozen—or hot—to think straight.

"Right," I say, and tear off my coat. I go for the buttons on my blouse, and my hands freeze in place. Should I go to the bathroom, or even to my grandparents' bedroom? I don't normally undress in front of others, and this is Jesse Freaking Campbell, who is turning my knees to soup.

"Do you need help?" he asks, and before I can answer, his big fingers start working the buttons on my shirt. "Good?" he asks once he finishes. I nod and slide the wet shirt from my shoulders standing before him in my bra and soaked yoga pants.

He tears off his coat, sweater and T-shirt, and once again I'm frozen in place. Have you ever watched cartoons as a child? There was this skunk, and his tongue would hang out and his eyes would bulge from his head when a pretty black and white female cat walked by. It was ridiculous and over the top, but I'm pretty sure I look like that skunk right now as I stare at Jesse's bare upper body as his hands go to the button on his jeans.

Okay, now that's the proper way a person makes a good first impression.

7

JESSE

I might be a red-blooded male who likes women, but I shouldn't be staring at Josie as she undresses. Then again, how could I not ogle the woman before me? She's gorgeous and sexy—don't even get me started on how those yoga pants are messing with my brain, not to mention the want in her eyes as she watches me strip. You know what else is messing with me? The goddamn sex sounds coming from the bedroom beside us. I'm going to kill Dane. But still. No. I shouldn't be staring because I'm a damn gentleman. Or at least I try to be.

I try to stop my teeth from chattering. I'm surprised I'm still shivering, actually. With the way my body is heating, I should be melting at this woman's feet.

"You should take your pants off," I say, and her mouth opens a little. Yeah, I think our frozen brains are taking us both down a sexual path. "I'll turn." I spin around and tug off my own pants, not an easy task when they're soaking wet, and grab up my drenched clothes. "Where should I put these?"

"Just...ugh...God, this is hard."

Now I can't help but want to hear her say those exact words with her body beneath mine.

"Bathroom?"

"Yes, ugh." She shuffles behind me and then gives a satisfied sigh. "Finally, got it."

Why does every single word coming out of her mouth make me think she's in the middle of a good orgasm and dammit, now I want to give her one. Only problem is, she's not the one-night stand kind of girl, according to Dane, and I don't want her to think there's more between us than there is. I'm with her so my buddy can get alone time with Kendra. Yeah, he's using this 'relationship' between Josie and me as an excuse to get together with a girl who's off limits, but whatever. He's my best friend and I owe him a thing or two for covering for me over the years.

"Shower?" I say as I step into the bathroom, grab a towel and pass it around my back to Josie. It takes everything in me not to turn around and look.

"There's only enough hot water for one, and the shower is pretty small."

I gesture with my head. "You take it then."

"I'm covered. You can turn." I spin to face her and her eyes are big and dark as she hugs the towel to her body. Christ, I've had a lot of women look at me over the years, but never quite with such vulnerability. My heart does a strange little spin.

"Come here." Dressed only in my boxers, I pull her body to mine, and use my heat to warm us. "Do you still have your underwear on?"

She gulps. "Yeah, why?"

I reach into the shower and turn the tap to hot. "Then it's like we're both in our bathing suits." I shrug to make light of it, and while I know we both need to warm up, I'm not entirely sure that's the only reason I'm suggesting we shower together. "No big deal, right?"

"No big deal," she agrees, and I step into the spray, pulling her in with me. She's right, the shower is small. Even alone in here, I'd have a hard time maneuvering. I put my arms around her, and since it's the only way we fit together, she does the same to me. Her hands are little, and when she splays her fingers, her touch does the strangest things to me. I've been touched a lot, but never with such curiosity and care. Her brand of tenderness is odd, and...nice. A quiver goes through her body and she moans in delight. Her sounds are fucking killing me.

I rest my head on hers, unable to put it anywhere else. "Doing okay, Josie?" I croak out.

"The cold is leaving my bones."

I really don't want to think about bones or what's happening with the one between my legs. "Yeah, me too," I manage to push past a tongue gone thick, and she shifts back a tiny inch, and lifts her head to see me. I smile down at her and brush her wet hair from her face. How did I never notice how pretty she was?

The first time I set eyes on her was when Dane and I visited the campus with his brother last Christmas. She never struck me as the kind of girl who went to frat parties, but there she was. I caught her looking at me, but she was gone before I could say hello, and while she's always quiet in the stands, I've seen her at the games. Afterward, she disappears, and I usually lose myself in some puck bunny.

"I'm sorry, Jesse," she murmurs quietly. "I don't even know what happened out there."

"I was getting tangled up, cursed out loud from frustration, and it startled you. You were worried something bad was happening to me, and lost your balance when you looked my way. I tried to help you and we both fell in."

She chuckles. "I guess that sums it up."

My hands leave her back and slide down, resting on the sexy curve just above her ass. I grind my teeth to stop myself from going further. I'm not interested in a knee to the nut sack. "You're kind of the hero in all this."

Her chuckle vibrates through me. "You're the one who rescued me," she points out.

"I guess we could look at it like that," I tease. I force my hands to her shoulders before I do something I might regret. "Wait, does that mean you now owe me your life, and you know, you're mine to do whatever I want with?"

Don't go there, Jesse.

She shifts, and her nipples pokes through her lace bra and presses against my chest. Jesus Christ. "I think the saying is, if you save a life, you're responsible for that life."

"Hmm, I think you might be right. Okay so I'm responsible for you now." I strangely like that idea even though it doesn't fit with my agenda: head down, all focus on hockey. "Could be worse."

"Could be worse?" she shoots back and playfully pinches my side.

"Hey." I wince and try to jump back but can't. "I didn't mean it that way. I mean, that doesn't sound so bad."

She angles her head, a small smile playing with the corners of her lips. "When talking about being responsible for me, I'm not sure 'not so bad' is better than 'could be worse' and believe me, I don't want to be anyone's burden."

"Never," I say. Since when did my words ever get tangled up around a woman before? I'm about to try to explain again, but stop when she speaks.

"I get what you mean, though, and you're not responsible for me. I'm a nursing student. I'm quite capable of taking care of myself." Her fingers trail down my back, and as she squares her shoulders to showcase strength, it's the vulnerability in her that does the strangest things to my heart. "In fact, I'm the one who takes care of others."

I search her face, and everything inside me softens when my gaze is met with warmth, and a hint of insecurity, something I suspect she's trying to hide, but here, nearly naked in the shower, it's pretty much impossible to conceal anything. My throat tightens in a way I'm not sure it's ever tightened before. Josie might be quiet and shy, but I have no doubt she *can* take care of herself. Everything about her tells me she's a nurturer by nature. She'd have to be to go into nursing, but I get the sense that she feels very much alone in this world.

Why is that?

My heart pinches, as the sudden need to be there for her claws at me. Perhaps it's because I have an older sister I'd do anything for, or perhaps it's because I have younger brothers that I've always looked after, but there's something happening inside me. Women have always just been for fun. They knew what they were getting into with me. My sole focus is hockey, and I can't lose that focus. I won't. I worked my ass off for years to get drafted and I can't let anything, or anyone stand in my way of playing for the Boston Bucks. Which makes this strange, new pull all that much more confusing. Maybe my brain really is frozen.

"Okay, how about this then? When you're in my territory, you're my responsibility and I'll take care of you."

"When will I be in your territory?"

"When you come to my farm to drive the tractor."

"Deal." She nods, but it's easy to tell she doesn't think that will ever happen.

She rests her cheek on my chest, and my heart pounds against it. As a nursing student, is she going to question my rapid heartbeat? Will she know it's pounding because I'm holding her tight, or will she blame it on our cold dunk?

I clear my throat. "This boat has that new boat smell."

"It's pretty new," she says, her voice tight, like she's bracing for something. Does she not want to talk about the boat?

"Do you have siblings?" I ask, changing the subject.

"No, it's just me. Do you?"

"Yeah, older sister and two younger brothers." Her eyes light up as she smiles up at me.

There's a longing in her voice when she says, "That sounds amazing."

I laugh and it comes out sounding rough and labored, thanks to the way she's running her fingers down my back. "Not as amazing as you'd think."

"Oh." She frowns, and I hate, absolutely fucking hate, that I somehow disappointed her.

"I love them and would kill for them. I'm just saying...family. Sometimes they can be a pain in the ass, you know." I shake my head. "No, I guess you don't know." She goes quiet, and the water grows cooler, but I'm not ready to leave the shower. I like being in here with her. It's warm, comfortable and intimate in ways I've never experienced before. "You wanted a brother or a sister?"

She snorts out a laugh. "I would have loved either. Mom and Dad were just always busy. I barely saw them growing up," she says, and I get the sense that she's telling me something very important, something very close to her heart. She snorts out a humorless laugh and looks around the posh bathroom. "I mean, I had material things, I just never had them." Her eyes go wide. "Ohmigod, I sound like—"

"You sound like someone who missed her parents." She swallows. "Were they nurses?" I ask.

"No, surgeons, actually."

"Ah, I see." She goes quiet and that's when I understand why I sensed loneliness in her. She might come from wealth, might even have been judged on that, but the neglect created hurt and longing inside her. "How about this? If you do visit the farm, my family is your family. They love to sit around the table at dinner time, and they're big and loud and will likely tell you horrible stories about me that aren't true, simply to make me look like an ass. They get a kick out of that."

Her grin wraps around my heart. "Fabricated?" She laughs. "Your family sounds amazing, and not at all like the kind of people who'd get a kick out of telling fake stories about you. There must be a shred of truth in them."

I arch a brow, and in my best serious voice ask, "Would I lie to you?"

"I don't know, Jesse." She smiles and it creates a new, deeper intimacy between us. "I don't know you very well."

"Yet here we are, nearly naked in the shower."

"Yeah," she agrees, the water getting colder by the second but neither of us seem to be in a hurry to move. "But no big deal, right?"

Since my cock has a mind of its own, it thickens between my legs and presses against her body and in the close quarters, there is absolutely nothing I can do to hide it.

What the fuck was that I just said about no big deal?

"I bet they're really proud of you," she says, so quietly I'm not even sure I heard her right.

"They are. I bet yours are proud of you too."

A noise crawls out of her throat and it's laced in sadness. "Yeah, they are." A beat of silence and then. "They would have preferred it if I followed in their footsteps. To them, nursing is a support role."

"Nurses do all the work, Josie. I have a huge respect for nurses."

Her smile is soft. "Thanks, but it'll never be good enough in their eyes." Under her breath she adds, "I'm always the side-kick, coming in second. Never anyone's number one." A heartbeat later, she opens her eyes wide and shakes her head. "I don't even know why I'm talking about this with you."

I kind of like that she is. "Hypothermia," I tell her. "It's like a truth serum." It's not, and she's a nursing student and knows that. I'm just trying to lighten her mood.

"Ah, so if I get you frozen again, you'll tell me all your secrets?"

"Is that what you were up to?" I tease, enjoying our easy banter. I like this girl, and she likes me too—according to Dane. But the reason I'm here tonight is to help my buddy out and I can't let her think there can be more between us. I should lay it all on the line, let her know what I'm all about. For some reason as she clings to me, I can't seem to spit out the words. "If I tell you my secrets, you'll have to tell me yours."

"Tit for tat," she says.

Fuck, I can't think about tit right now, or I'm going to put my mouth on the ones pressing against me. The boat rocks and we simply hold on to one another, until I'm worried we're going to get hypothermia again.

"We should get out. You're starting to shiver," I say.

"Yeah."

I make a move a contortionist would be proud of and twist and turn off the nozzle. The water slows, and I open the door and step out, but the only problem is, I slip on the water that seeped out from the shower door and land on my back, Josie toppling down with me, and that's when all the blood leaves my brain, and I cup the back of her neck and bring her mouth to mine.

8

JOSIE

I'm a bundle of freaking nerves sitting next to Jesse in the back seat of Dane's vehicle. Am I really going to his farm? He teased that he'd teach me to drive a tractor in exchange for teaching him how to pilot a boat, which we never got around to doing. But I didn't think he was serious. Yet here I am, heading to Bass River with him, Dane, and my best friend, Kendra.

"Carter's family also does a haunted house and a haunted corn maze," Jesse tells Kendra joining in the conversation coming from the front seat as I sit here in the back with Jesse, resisting the urge to pinch myself.

Kendra turns to see him. "No way."

Dane grins at Kendra. "We'll go tomorrow."

Her eyes go wide. "It's okay if we don't."

Dane laughs and I pipe in. "I actually think that would be fun."

"Let's do it," Jesse says, and I steal a fast glance at the man beside me and try not to have a panic attack. I've seen him since that night we showered together, and kissed deeply, passionately on the small bathroom floor of the boat. We haven't kissed since, haven't really been alone like that. When we go out, we're always 'double-dating', and once again, I am not even sure what we're doing could be called dating.

He offers me a smile that melts my insides despite the cool October air. Will we share a bed at his farmhouse? Maybe the better question is, do I want to?

Yes, God yes, I want to.

Like I said, I'm not sure what is going on with us. I do however notice the glances he casts my way when he thinks I'm not looking, even at the rink after a game. Trust me, I'm always looking. Jesse is hard not to look at which reminds me how much he's loved by the puck bunnies, and once again makes me wonder, why me?

I'm not sure, and I'm not sure I want to delve too deeply into that. I'm a worrier, an overthinker, yet, for some reason, I just want to enjoy every minute with him and let nature take its course without wondering if this is going anywhere. If someone put a gun to my head and demanded an answer on that, I think I'd say yes, we're going somewhere—based on the way he looks at me. A little bubble of excitement mingles with the nervousness, and I look straight ahead as Dane pulls the car off the road and a big old farmhouse rises up in the distance.

"Wow, it's so big," I say.

Dane chuckles. "That's what cheese says."

"What?" I ask.

"Ignore him," Kendra says. Dane comes from a family of artisanal cheese makers, so I guess that's an inside joke.

Jesse reaches over and gives my hand a squeeze. Does he sense my apprehension? Meeting his family feels like it's kind of a big deal, and I guess I really want them to like me. I really want a lot of things this weekend, actually.

Jesse's mother steps outside to greet us, and she's warm and welcoming, her arms spread to bring me in, and I instantly bond with her. I breathe in the scent of cinnamon as she hugs me tightly. My chest expands, longing for a loving family like this. If I ever have kids, I plan to be a big part of their life, and perhaps I chose to be a nurse over a surgeon so I wouldn't have to work all hours. It wasn't much fun being raised by a nanny. I hope that doesn't sound like a spoiled rich girl problem.

As if privy to my inner thoughts, Jesse's hand lands on my back, a comforting rub on my shoulder blade. For a guy who is tough as nails on the ice, he's kind of a softie deep down and I'm enjoying getting to know this side of him.

"It's so nice to meet you, Mrs. Campbell." For a second I almost call her Mrs. Soup. God, I really am nervous, even though I shouldn't be. I think we're going to all get along just fine.

"Please call me Carol."

We all wave Dane and Kendra off, and catching me by surprise, Jesse takes my hand and leads me into his house. He gives it a squeeze and offers me a reassuring smile. He's really come to know and understand my anxieties in such a short time.

"I'll make us some coffee and get your father."

His younger brothers come racing down the stairs, clamoring for Jesse's attention, but stop abruptly when they see me.

"Oh hey," the younger one says.

"What, you've never seen a girl before?" Jesse teases and puts him in a headlock. "Josie, this is Jaxon."

"Hey," the older boy says, playing it cool and running his hands through his hair, much like Jesse does.

"And this is Justin."

We all exchange pleasantries, and for the briefest of seconds, as his brothers fight for his attention, telling him all the things they want to do this weekend, I wonder if I should be here. I inch back a bit, about to retreat into myself, when Jesse captures my hand. It's crazy how well he can read me. That's probably what makes him a great hockey player.

"Let's take our stuff to our room."

His brother's grumble as Jesse tells them what we have planned this weekend—mainly meeting up with Kendra and Dane for the haunted house and haunted corn maze—and goes on to reassure them he'll hang out with them later. We head upstairs, and he guides me to his bedroom. Our bags land with a thump on his bedroom floor, and I turn at the sound.

The second my gaze shifts to his and I see heat and hunger, my heart jumps into my throat. I take a fast breath as he takes two big steps and closes the distance between us. My blood fires, the temperature in the room jumping a few degrees as he pulls me to him and puts his lips on mine, like it's been something he's been thinking about for a very long time.

I kiss him back, melting against his body as the intimacy in our relationship goes from zero to six million in two seconds. His tongue tangles with mine, and he puts his hand on the back of my neck, angling me, his tongue plays and tastes the depts of me.

My God, I never thought our kisses could be hotter than that first one on the floor of the boat, but I was wrong, and I'm so happy about that. He grunts into my mouth and the deep, needy guttural sound sends heat through my body. It settles between my legs and my sex tingles, wanting so much more... everything. His cock presses against my body and for a split second I think he's going to lay me out on his bed and have his way with me, until his mother's voice sounds from downstairs.

"Coffee is ready."

Jesse breaks the kiss, and his face is tortured as he gazes at me. "Do you have any idea how long I've wanted to do that?" he asks, as he takes a harsh breath.

"Why haven't you?"

Something dark, almost pained and confused moves over his face, like he's fighting a demon only he can see. "We haven't been alone."

No, we haven't. Every time we go out, we're with Dane and Kendra. "I'm looking forward to alone time this weekend," I tell him, wanting him to know exactly where I am in this relationship.

"Yeah, me too." He angles his head as dishes clang downstairs. His shoulders sag and he exhales. "Ready to hear all the horrible stories about me?"

I laugh as he teases. "Jesse, they all adore you. It's easy to see that."

He perks up. "Mom already loves you. We all..." his words fall off and omigod, what was he going to say. "We should go."

I nod. "Wait, are we sharing this room?" My heart lurches, excited by the idea of being in his bed with him, but with his family in the house...

He frowns and my heart drops. "As much as I want that, parents, my younger siblings...I have to be a good big brother and set a good example."

"I understand that."

He grins, like he has something up his sleeve, and before I can ask, he takes my hand to lead me downstairs, and I sort of love the way he keeps doing that. Like I'm his girl and he wants me close. We head down to find his mother and father in the kitchen. Carol takes a tray of muffins from the oven, and before anyone can introduce me to Jesse's father, his brother comes running in as delicious smells fill the kitchen.

Justin reaches for one, and Carol slaps his hand. He yelps and tugs it back. "Guests first, Justin."

He grumbles under his breath as Carol places a muffin on a plate and hands it to him. "Please give this to Josie."

He turns to Jesse and grins. "Can I sit by her too?"

"Over there, little brother." He points, and I grin at their playfulness, and glance at Jesse as he drops down next to me and shifts closer in a possessive manner. I'm not sure what is going on with him this weekend—maybe it has to do with the fact that we're finally going to have some alone time, but I like it. I like it so much I want more of this Jesse.

Justin laughs as he circles the table and plunks down. Carol sets a plate of muffins on the table, and he snatches one up. Jaxon comes racing in and has half a muffin gone before he even sits down. I catch Mr. Campbell's eye, and it's easy to see how much he adores his boys. It fills me with warmth and longing.

"Is your sister here?" I ask.

Carol frowns. "Unfortunately, no. She couldn't get home this weekend."

Jesse leans in and tells me she's in the States, playing college hockey.

"How about you two?" I ask Jesse's brothers. "You guys play?"

"Yup," Justin says. "We still having the pick-up game this weekend?" he asks Jesse.

Jesse pops a piece of muffin in his mouth. "You can count on it."

"Then be prepared to have your ass handed to you, big brother," Jaxon says as he holds his hand up to Justin for a high five.

"Language," Carol says, and sips her coffee, but she's smiling and enjoying her family all together at the table. My heart tumbles, loving everything about this.

"Bring it," Jesse says and reaches for his coffee, his eyes on his brother. I have no doubt Jesse is a good big brother, and does his best to set high standards for his siblings.

Jaxon laughs. "Remember that time..."

"Oh, God no," Jesse says, and buries his face in his hands. "No stories."

I smile and clap my hands. "Oh, please, lots of stories."

"There was this one time Jesse set our shed on fire." Jaxon holds his hands up. "Don't worry, no cows were injured from his stupidity."

"Remember," Jesse says and looks at me. "Lies."

"Are you saying you didn't burn the shed down?" I query.

"Well...no..."

I laugh and beneath the table his hand lands on my knee, and the warmth it creates wraps around my heart and squeezes. I honestly never believed in insta-love until now. We've been hanging out, but something is happening here, something deep and profound and I think he feels it every bit as much as I do.

I really hope I'm not wrong here, or I'm going to be in a lot of trouble.

JESSE

I take Josie's hand as we walk toward the haunted corn maze, and my heart thunders in my chest. The way everything inside me is reacting to her is crazy. I've been with numerous women, but none of them have ever thrown me off my game before, and the truth is, I can't let anything, or anyone distract me from my future. It could ruin everything I've worked so hard for.

"Are you okay?" she asks, and I turn to her. Is she sensing the struggling inside of me? Fuck, man, I'm not supposed to fall for a girl.

Ah, but there's something very special about this one, dude.

That realization hits like a puck to the face and nearly takes the wind out of me. I swallow as my throat tightens, and stare at the woman who managed to find her way under my armor without even trying. Christ, I must be mistaken. I can't be falling for her. The truth is, I haven't known her that long. Certainly not long enough to want more than casual fun, and

I do not believe in love at first sight. Or second. Or...you get the gist.

Fuck me, twice.

"I'm good. Scared of what's going to jump out at me in the haunted maze," I tease and feign a shiver.

She laughs and bumps into me. "I'll protect you," she tells me even though she knows I've been to the haunted maze so many times, I could run through with my eyes closed.

I toss my arm around her and pull her close. As her body melts against mine, my heart once again thumps hard. Yeah, this can't be good. We step inside the corn maze and I glance around. I want Josie all to myself tonight and there are far too many people here for my liking.

"Can I show you something?" I ask.

She arches a brow, as a grin I have no control over parts my lips. "I suppose," she says, suspicion in her voice.

"Come on." I take her hand and we leave the maze. I guide her around back to the barn at the far end of the property. I've been in this barn numerous times, helping my buddy Carter out with his chores when we were younger.

I push the door open, and use my phone's flashlight app to glance around. Maybe someone else has the same idea as I do. I really don't want to see anyone's naked ass. Not entirely true. I want to see Josie's.

"Anyone here?" I call out. Josie snuggles up behind me, putting her arms around my waist as her breasts press into my back. I put my hand over hers, and run my thumb over her soft skin. "I think we're alone," I whisper to her when no one answers my call.

"Finally," she says, her quiver vibrating through my body and letting me know she wants to be with me as much as I want to be with her. Fuck, last night, knowing she was in my bed was torturous. I laid awake in the guest room and had to talk myself out of sneaking in and sliding between her legs, but I'd never want to disrespect my parents like that. This is their house and I follow their rules.

But now, inside this barn, I can finally do what I've been fantasizing about in my campus bed for weeks now. "Let's go up."

I take her hand and tug and she follows me to the ladder leading to the hay loft.

"I've never been in a hay loft before," she says quietly.

I tuck my phone away, and moonlight shines in from the rafters. "You don't have hay allergies, do you?"

"I don't think so." She glances at me over her shoulder, and I catch her teasing grin. "I do feel a bit flushed though. Is that a symptom of hay fever?"

I make a hissing sound, insinuating flushed skin could be catastrophic. "That's not good." She goes up a few more steps, and her sweet ass is right there in front of my face. My cock thickens in my jeans, and I ache to free it. "Are you feeling hot?"

"Very," she says, her voice a little higher, her breath coming a little faster. She reaches the loft, sits on a bale of hay as I climb, and puts her hands on her cheeks. "I think I might be burning up." I reach the loft, take her hand and pull her to her feet. Her body collides with mine. "What other symptoms should I look for?"

I slide my hand down her body to cup her ass. I pull her against my hard cock and she moans. The sound curls around me and strokes the long hard length of my dick. "Your throat, is it scratchy, dry?" I ask.

"Yes," she murmurs, and the needy sound massages my balls. "Is it dangerous?"

"Could be," I tell her, loving this intimate little game we're playing.

She blinks at me. "What should I do about that?"

"Probably find a way to moisten it."

"I was thinking the same thing." Grinning, her hands go to my button and she pops it. This time I'm the one moaning. "Sounds like you might have a few symptoms yourself," she says her voice laced with arousal. She pulls my zipper down and is about to sink to her knees. Fuck, as much as I want her sweet lips around my cock, I have to get my mouth on her first. I've been aching to pleasure her, hear my name on her tongue as I bring her to climax.

I put my hand on her wrist to stop her and her eyes meet mine. In the past, I would have let a girl blow me first, but I want to do right by her and pleasure her first. I slide my hand between her legs, and rub her through her yoga pants. Does she have any idea what her tight little body-hugging yoga pants have been doing to me? Her little gasp fills the silence in the barn.

"Jesse," she moans and my chest swells, loving the need in her voice as she says my name.

She lifts her face to mine and I tug the band of her pants from her belly and slide my hand inside. She gasps again, and

I put my mouth on hers to silence her. As much as I want this woman to scream for me, I don't need anyone running in here to see what the commotion is all about.

I dip into her panties and she's so goddamn wet I nearly lose my fucking mind. "Josie," I murmur. "You're so wet."

"Another symptom?" she asks, her voice breaking as I circle her clit with my finger.

"Oh yeah." It's a symptom all right. A symptom from wanting to be with me, and I can't even believe how happy that makes me.

"You're a farm boy, do you know the remedy?"

She moves her body, seeking my finger and I oblige, wanting to give this woman everything. I inch a finger into her sopping wet pussy, and her muscles ripple. Jesus, she's so close. My cock throbs in response, wanting to sink high inside her. She rocks against me and my mouth dries, aching to taste her.

"I'm pretty sure I do." I sink to my knees and tug her pants down. Her hands go to my shoulders and she holds on as I peel her pants and panties from her body. Once I have her half naked, I tear off my jacket, and lay it out on the hay bale. "Sit," I command.

She drops down, and I grip her thighs and widen her legs. "Oh God," she murmurs as I lean forward and bury my face in her wet pussy. The first sweet taste of her sends heat and need rocketing through my body. I dive in deeper, putting my tongue inside her, wanting her taste on my tongue Sunday, a week from tomorrow. No, that's not exactly true. I want her taste on my tongue forever. Jesus, what am I saying? Knowing I want her this much is fucking scary.

You can't fall for her, Jesse.

With that thought in mind, I slide a finger in her as I tongue her clit, struggling to make this all about sex. She moans and writhes against me, and I pay attention to her reactions as I fuck her with my finger and tongue. As I learn her body, my cock throbs for attention, but I need her cum on my tongue before I sink my dick into her.

Her breathing changes, and I apply a little more pressure to her clit, sliding my finger in and out of her a bit faster until she breaks around me, her sweet, sweet cum spilling into my mouth. My groan of pleasure mingles with hers, and it's the most harmonic sound I've ever heard.

"Babe," I say as I lift my head, and find her gaze locked on mine. "You taste so good."

She grabs the back of my head and brings my mouth to hers. "Show me," she says, her hot words nearly bringing me to climax. I kiss her, hardly able to believe how much this quiet, shy girl has come to life, has let go of her inhibitions under my touch. She moans, and my chest swells as I slide my tongue into her mouth.

Her hand slides between our bodies and she opens my zipper. Her small hand wraps around my throbbing cock and as she strokes me, I can't believe how close I am to losing my load.

"Babe," I say and the next thing I know, I'm on my back on the floor, and she's tugging my cock free. Her sweet mouth closes over my crown, and suddenly I'm the one who can't stay quiet. I grunt, and grip a fistful of her hair as she takes me to the back of her throat. Heaven. Sweet fucking heaven —a place no girl has ever taken me to before. It's bright and colorful, and so damn sweet, I never want to leave.

Do you have to leave, Jesse?

She sucks me, and I clench down to stop myself from spurting down her throat. I grunt and groan and fist her hair in my hands, needing to stop this as much as I need it to continue. I swell in her mouth and the erotic sound she makes nearly shatters me.

"Babe," I say, and ease her off my dick. "I need my cock inside you."

"Yes," she moans. I tug a condom from my pants, and then pull them, as well as my shirt off. I make a bed with our jackets and lay her on it. I climb over her and when she wraps her arms around my body, it feels like this is where I belong, where I was always meant to be.

My lips find hers, and as anxious and needy as I am, I want to draw this out. I have no idea if our first time will also be our last.

"I want you," I straight up tell her. The smile that comes over her face, hugs my heart.

"I want you too, Jesse."

With that, I slide into her and her head rolls to the side, our low moans once again mingling. As her muscles hug my cock, I push deep, wanting every inch of myself inside her. She wraps her legs around me as I fuck her, our bodies meant for each other. I'm not sure sex has ever been this good for me. What the fuck is happening?

It's different because you really like this girl, Jesse.

I block that thought and try to concentrate only on the pleasure but the thing is, the pleasure is better when I'm not blocking the warmth and love inside me.

Love?

We cling to one another, both giving and taking, and as I pump into her, her sweet body opening and welcoming all of me, my climax builds. I hold on, wanting to bring her to orgasm again, desperate to feel her muscles clench around my cock. I angle my body for deeper thrusts and put my finger on her clit, applying the pressure that took her to completion moments ago.

"Jesse," she cries out, her nails clawing at my back as wet heat floods from her body and singes my cock, pulling my orgasm from me.

"Fuck, Josie. Fuck." I kiss her as we tumble into bliss and no matter how hard I try to keep my heart out of this, the truth of the matter is that I can't. Letting the emotions flood me, makes everything so much better. My kisses slow as our climaxes subside, and I inch back to see the satiated look on her face. It's the most beautiful thing I've ever seen.

"Hey," I whisper and slide off her, giving her a break from my weight. My cock instantly misses her warmth.

She jokingly says, "I guess I can check sex in a hay loft off my bucket list."

We both laugh quietly, and go silent as we simply touch each other's bodies. I run my fingers down her arms, wanting to explore her more, and she touches my chest, the soft pad of her finger circling my nipple.

After a long moment, she sneezes, and then laughs. "Hay fever," she tells me, her voice a bit hoarse.

I grin and roll on top of her, wanting her again and again and again, despite the fact that it's not conducive to my plan to put all my focus on hockey.

"Good thing we know the remedy," I say, knowing full well that if I spend more time with her, inside her, it's going to fuck me up big time.

The air is cool, the semester passing by quickly, and while the boats should be put away by now, I promised Jesse I'd teach him to pilot one and, since the lake at our cottage isn't frozen yet, I plan to do just that. Honestly, I'm kind of glad Kendra and Dane didn't want to come on the boat with us. Jesse and I have very little alone time.

Sure, when we were at his childhood home ages ago, we did have time to ourselves, but when it comes right down to it, we technically went to Bass River with our friends, just like we're here at my family cottage with them right now. I get the sense that Jesse wants to spend quiet time with me; we just never go anywhere without Kendra and Dane, and I'd like to change that.

As Jesse takes the wheel and steers the boat to the middle of the lake after I gave him a quick lesson, I stand close and watch, ready to jump in and help if he needs it, but he's a quick study on so many levels and he's quite capable of handling this boat without any interference. He turns my way and his grin is so big, it wraps around my heart and squeezes. I know it's only been a few months since we've been hanging out, but there's no denying it. I want this man. Heck, Christmas will be here before we know it, and even though I'm not close to my parents, I'd love to introduce Jesse to them.

Jesse will be going home for the holidays, and I love that he's so close to his family. Maybe he'll want me to go with him. My stomach flutters at the idea of sitting around a big tree opening gifts and laughing over hot chocolate. Yes, I've clearly watched too many Hallmark movies. Is that a standard that can be reached? I'm not sure. All I know is I want that with the man who's grinning like a kid on Christmas morning.

"Having fun?" I ask.

"You know it." He winks at me. "When I grow up, I want a boat like this."

I shrug. "We can use this one anytime we want."

His smile falls so fast, a burst of worry flushes my blood. What did I say? Is he not thinking about a future like I am? Maybe I'm overthinking and he just wants a boat of his own.

I step up to him and put my hand on his back. There's warmth in his gaze as he turns to me, and it ebbs the unease inside me.

He gestures with a nod. "Want to go over there, to the secluded cove?"

I grin, guessing what he has in mind. "Sure."

He turns the boat and once we're in the cove he asks, "Want to drop anchor?"

I nod. "Want me to teach you?"

"Yup."

For the next few minutes, I show him how to drop anchor and explain the difference between fluke and plow anchors and show him how we determine the depths. I love the way he listens so carefully. Once we secure the boat, he pulls me to him and glances at the sky.

"Can we sleep out here?"

"It might get cold."

"If I promise to keep you warm, will you say yes?" he asks, his voice eager, his eyes hopeful and full of heat.

I grin, pretty sure I'd say yes to anything this man suggests. "How exactly do you plan to keep me warm?"

He tugs down the zipper on my jacket. "First, we'll have to remove this."

I arch a brow. "I'm not sure removing my clothes is the best way to warm me."

He takes my hand and we step back inside the cabin of the boat. He pushes my coat from my shoulders, and then shrugs out of his. "You're going to have to trust me on this, Josie."

Trust...

Do I trust Jesse? Yes, I totally do and trust doesn't come that easily to me. But he has never given me a reason not to trust him.

"Okay," I say. "I trust you."

He goes still for the briefest of seconds, an almost spooked look in his eyes. It disappears as quickly as it appeared. Did I imagine it or is something strange going on with him tonight? I'm about to ask, but he slides his big hands under my sweater, and brings me close. My worried thoughts evaporate as his mouth lands on mine, and that's when I realize tonight is for pleasure, not talking. But the truth is, I want more, which means soon we're going to have to have a conversation.

"Arms up," he commands in that sexy voice that arouses me, and I quickly oblige. My body quakes as he peels my sweater off. Partly because it knows what's to come, and partly because it's been far too long since we've been alone together. I want to change that. I want more time in his arms—naked—not just when we're out with our friends and they go off together. I want us to be together for no other reason than we want to be together. Sometimes I feel like Kendra and Dane's support cast, their sidekicks, and in my heart, I want to be this man's number one. Is that asking too much? I'm not sure, because everything in the way he looks at me with adoration, and touches me with heat and hunger, I don't think it is too much.

He growls as he drops my sweater to the floor and I stand before him in my bra and yoga pants. Yes, I know how much he loves my curve-hugging pants and yes, I wore them tonight on purpose.

"I've missed these," he says, and unhooks my bra to take my breasts into his big palms. "I never got to spend enough time here." He bends and takes one nipple into his mouth and I groan, throw my head back and rake my fingers through his hair. He licks and nibbles and sucks until the sensations barrelling through my body settle deep between my legs. My sex moistens, and I rock against him, needing him to fill me. Now.

"Need something, babe?" he asks around my nipple, and I whimper and put my hand on his cock, thrilled to find him rock hard and ready.

You do this to him, Josie.

That thought thrills me, and my heart thunders as I rub him. "I don't think I'm the only one who needs something," I respond, and he pushes against my hand as he moves his mouth to my other nipple. Every lick takes my pleasure to new heights, and my mouth waters to taste him.

"Could this be what you need?" I ask, putting my hands on his shoulders to push him back an inch.

There's confusion on his face, but it quickly morphs to hunger as I drop to my knees and free his engorged cock. I take him into my mouth, savoring the tangy pre-cum as he grunts and juts his hips forward. I really love the way he responds to me.

I suck him deep and take his balls into my palm and he thickens even more. "Josie," he moans, and the tortured sound teases my sex, and I take him a little deeper, loving the way he's becoming unhinged under my ministrations.

He grips my hair and tugs, and dammit I don't want to stop. I want this man to come in my mouth, and one of these days I plan to make it happen. Right now, however, I think he's anxious to be inside me, and hey, I'd like to give the man what he wants. Okay, fine, I want it too.

He helps me to my feet and I expect him to take me to the bedroom, but he doesn't. I take in the primal hunger on his face as he turns me and bends me over the galley table. Oh my.

"I want you like this so I can bury myself in you, babe," he says, his mouth near my ear as he presses his cock against my ass. I hear the foil crinkle as he rips into a condom and quickly sheathes himself. "I want my cock as deep as it can go and I'm not even sure that's going to be enough for me."

A hard quiver goes through my body as the need in his voice falls over me. "Yes, please..." My God is that my voice. I don't know. I only know I love the way he wants me and makes me feel like I'm the most special woman in the world—like I'm actually not the supporting cast, I'm the lead, this man's number one.

He tugs my yoga pants and panties down and once I'm naked, he gently kicks my feet apart to widen my legs. As I spread, my sex opens for him, begging to be filled.

"Jesus," he hisses as he goes to his knees and licks my pussy. He slides a finger in, and I moan as my muscles lightly clench around him. I can't believe I'm so close. Maybe I can, I've been wanting to get naked with him again for a very long time.

He stands to his full height and bends over me, putting his hands over mine as his rock-hard cock presses against my opening. "Ready for me?" he asks, and I suck in a breath. At first, I wasn't sure I was ready for a guy like Jesse. I'm not a puck bunny. Heck, I wasn't even on his radar. Now, however, I think I am ready for a guy like him.

"Yes. Are you ready for me?" I ask, knowing he's astute enough to read between the lines.

For the briefest of seconds, he stops breathing, and just when I'm about to turn my head to check on him, he slides into me, answering my question—just not the one I was really asking—with his body. I'll think about that later, though, when he's not filling me with his beautiful thick cock and rocketing me into outer space.

He grunts, removes his hand from mine to grip my hips for leverage. "Babe," he groans, pushing hard and deep and hitting me in places that pull a scream from my lungs. "Yes," he says, the sound clearly thrilling him.

With no need to be quiet, I chant his name as he rocks into me, and the boat sways with the movements. He fucks me, long deep strokes that quickly sends us catapulting into outer space. I come around his cock, and he pushes deep and releases inside me. I revel in each glorious pulse, never wanting the night to end. His breath is ragged, hot on my back and I whimper as satisfaction rolls through me.

His smile is warm and sated as he picks me up and pulls me to him. I run my fingers through his damp hair. "I thought you said I could trust you," I tease. His smile falls, and my heart jumps, at the hurt moving into his eyes. Oh no, I didn't mean to upset him. I hurry to say, "You said getting me naked would warm me."

He blinks, his eyes still confused. "You're not warm?"

"No," I tell him, and as he puts his hands on my arms, rubbing to create friction, my heart melts. Could this man be any sweeter? God, I am so lost in him and dammit, he came at me with his A-game, giving me a winning orgasm and I still want him again.

He swallows like it's painful. "I can get you a blanket."

I chuckle. "Jesse, what I'm trying to say is, maybe we should get a glass of water, crawl into my bed, and see about heating things up again."

A huge smile spreads across his face. "Ah, I get it. You were playing with me. Clearly after an orgasm, you have to spell things out for me." He taps his head. "No blood left in the brain."

"S. E. X."

The next thing I know I'm laughing as he picks me up, and carries me to my bed. We fall into it together, and once again he makes me feel like I'm his number one, and nothing can come between us. As I revel in that, something niggles in the back of my brain, something about the odd way he acted at certain times tonight.

Is he not as into me as I am into him? Am I reading this all wrong?

11

JESSE

"Y**ou look like you need to talk,"** a freshly showered Dane says to me as I stand outside his dorm room, while he tugs on his socks.

"What makes you say that?" I ask and scrub my face, noting that he too seems a bit off today. "Actually, you look like you want to talk, too."

"I do, but first I want to hear what's going on with you."

I wish I knew what the fuck was going on with me. I spent my whole life focused on hockey and hooking up on the weekends, and now being with anyone other than Josie, has zero appeal. Fuck, I wasn't supposed to fall for her.

Oh, but you did, buddy, you did.

The truth is, I thought a relationship would take my focus from hockey, but in fact it's enhanced it. I'm happier now, fulfilled in so many ways. Knowing she's in the stands cheering me on makes me a better player. I turn the conversation back to Dane. "So you and Kendra, are you still sneaking around?"

"For now, but she's going to talk to her brother."

I shake my head, "Good, glad to hear it. I'm tired of all this bullshit."

"Once her brother knows, we'll no longer need you to pretend you're with Josie, and that Kendra and I are your sidekicks, tagging along to keep you two company when really it's the other way around."

I snort. "About fucking time you two got your shit together."

"You're right, and now you can go back to hooking up every weekend." He arches his brow, his lips quirked. Fuck my buddy knows me so well, I guess he can tell I've fallen for Josie and is waiting for me to admit it.

"You and Kendra owe me big time for being a part of this ridiculous ruse." I'm kidding, they don't. I got more out of this than I ever bargained for. I mean, sure I was doing it to help out my buddy, but I discovered Josie was sweet, and vulnerable and kind and how could I not fall for a girl like that?

A noise sounds behind me and I push off the door and turn to catch a glimpse of someone's dark ponytail bouncing as they race down the stairs. Was that Josie? My heart jumps into my throat. "Fuck."

"What?"

I turn back to Dane as he pushes off his bed. "I think that was Josie."

"Why do you look like you've seen a ghost?"

"What if she heard you?" I swallow and try not to panic. If I hurt Josie, I'd never forgive myself. "What if she thinks I was only hanging out with her so you could be with Kendra?"

"You were, weren't you?" he asks, pushing me to admit how I feel.

"Yes...no...fuck."

"Shit, buddy, you've got it bad, stop denying it or fighting it. Being with her hasn't fucked with your concentration on the ice, it's made it better. I knew from the beginning once you got to know her, you'd like her." Dane pushes past me and walks into the hall. He leans over the rail and glances down the stairs. "You'd better go after her."

I try to quiet my thundering heart, but can't. What the fuck have I done? "You think she'll even talk to me again after that?" I ask, unable to keep my voice from shaking. I shove my hands into my pockets and remove them again, fisting and un-fisting my fingers, my anxiety making me antsy.

"There's only one way to find out."

I nod, and hurry to my room. I grab my winter coat and run outside, nearly slipping on the falling snow. I look for foot-prints, but the snow is coming so fast now, it's covering all traces of her. I run back upstairs to Dane's room.

I'm breathless when I ask, "Can you call Kendra, see if she knows where Josie is?"

Dane grabs his phone and calls his girl. They talk for a few minutes, and he hangs up. "Kendra said she was coming here to surprise you with pizza."

"Fuck, it was her." Panic grips my stomach and it's all I can do not to vomit. "I need to find her. Where would she be?" I practically scream, my words all running together as my head throbs.

"It's snowing. She's probably going home."

"Right."

I turn to go find out. Dane grabs his coat. "I'll come with you."

We hop in his car, and I glance up and down the streets. The homes are decorated for the holiday season, and as of right now, with worry racing through my blood, I have zero Christmas spirit. I can't fucking believe Josie overheard us and now thinks I was using her. We've grown so close, and I have no doubt she cares for me as much as I care for her. She must be so fucking hurt. A groan crawls out of my throat.

Dane glances at me. "It'll be okay, buddy."

I shake my head, not sure how it will be. We reach Kendra's place and hurry inside, but Josie is nowhere to be found. We all message her, and I pace as we all wait, but no response comes to any of us.

How can I make this right? How can I prove to her that I love her, and that she's the most important person in the world to me? She talked to me about always feeling like a supporting cast member, but she's not to me. She's the main character, the number one person in my life. How can I prove that now after what she just overheard?

I take in a breath, but can hardly fill my lungs. "I have to go find her."

Dane and Kendra simply nod, and I step outside. As I run back to the dorm, trying to figure out where I might find Josie, an idea hits. I hurry back to my room and tear open my closet. I find what I'm looking for and grab a black marker. Once I'm satisfied, I message Josie again. When she still doesn't answer, I wrack my brain. Where would she be?

I head back outside and search the streets. After hours, I go back to the dorm, plop down on my bed, and my stomach is in knots as the hours tick by. Soon enough I fall into a fitful sleep, and I wake to a white winter wonderland outside. I check my phone and a heavy wave of disappointment squeezes the air from my lungs. Christ, where is she? Maybe I'll find her on campus.

I spend the day searching for her, and skipping my own classes. But she's nowhere to be found and no one has seen her, not even Kendra. Of course, she'd be mad at Kendra too. Kendra knew Josie liked me and Josie must believe her friend took advantage of that. The only saving grace is that Dane and Kendra thought I'd fall for her in return, and I did.

Soon enough nighttime blankets the city, and I head back to the dorm. Christmas music blares from the kitchen when I enter Storm House, and one of the guys is decorating a tree in the main room. I'm in no mood for that. I go to my room, worry gripping me. Where the hell is Josie? A new kind of panic invades my body. What if she's physically hurt herself and can't message anyone?

That's when it hits me. There's only one place she could be, and I'm pretty sure I know where that is. I snatch up the gift I made to show her exactly what she means to me.

Outside, I leave my car and head straight to the waterfront. I run the long length of it until I come to her grandfather's boat. I check the chain to find it locked and hop over it. I see a light burning inside and I take a fast, relieved breath, happy she's safe.

I jump on the boat, and knock on the small door. "Josie, it's me. Can I come in?" At first my words are met with silence, and I knock again. "Please, Josie. It's not what you think."

Her voice comes through the door. "Are you telling me Kendra and Dane weren't using us so they could be together, and you knew and went along with it?"

The pain in her voice slices through me like a sharpened skate blade, and it's almost impossible to breathe. "I once asked you to trust me, Josie. I'm asking for you to trust me again. Can I please come in and explain?" A moment passes and then the door opens. The second I set eyes on Josie and see that she's been crying because I'd hurt her, I clench down on my jaw. My chest aches as I fight back a sob.

She backs up and sits on the small sofa, like her legs are ready to give out and I hurry to her. "Kendra set us up because she knew you liked me, and Dane thought I'd like you. Their intentions were good, but yes, you're right, they did take advantage of the situation. I allowed it because I owed Dane."

She sniffs and gives a humorless laugh. "I should have known I was part of the supporting cast. I am such a fool."

"Want to know why else I allowed it?" Before she can say no, or kick me out, I pull my jersey from my bag, and hold it out to her. She stares at it, completely confused.

"Why did you black out the nine?" she asks quietly.

"I'm number nineteen on the team." I point to the bright white number one, which is not blacked out. "I want you to have this because this is what you are to me, and I never want you to forget that." She glances at the number one on the back of the jersey and her eyes grow wide.

"Jesse…"

"I'm in love with you, Josie. I fought it, I really did. I was worried, terrified love would interfere with my game, and my career goals. I was so fucking wrong. Everything about you compliments me, makes me a better player, and you're not the fool. I was a fool for fighting it, for not telling you right away how I felt."

Tears flood her eyes. "You love me?"

"Yes, I fucking love you." I drop to my knees in front of her and pull her to me. I hold her tight, and my heart thunders. "I…I'm scared, Josie."

"You just said loving me makes you a better player."

I glance at her. "I never meant to hurt you, and I'm so fucking scared I've lost you."

A small smile touches her mouth, and she glances around the boat. "You found me."

"Don't ever disappear on me again." I cup her cheeks and kiss her deeply to let her know what she means to me. "Come home with me for Christmas."

She sniffs as happy tears fall from her eyes. "I would love that."

My heart jumps with happiness, thrilled that we're going to be okay. "You would?"

I take in the joy on her face, the brightness in her glossy eyes. "Yes, I would, because I love you too, Jesse."

I sneeze. I'm probably getting sick from running around outside in the cold. "Oh no. Do you have boat allergies?" she teases.

"I might," I say, knowing where she's going with this and loving it. "You're the captain of this boat. Do you know the remedy?"

She grins, and unzips my coat. "I believe I do, Jesse. I believe I do."

Christmas Morning:

My heart is so full I fear it's going to burst as I sit around a big, beautifully decorated Christmas tree with Jesse's family, along with Kendra and Dane. We're all in Bass River for the holiday's and I have never felt so at home, or so much love in one room.

I catch Kendra's eye and smile at her. She smiles back. I was so angry when I found out what was going on behind the scenes, but after we talked it out the other day, and I found out what she was going through—I feel bad that I wasn't there for her because her life was in complete turmoil—we hugged it out, and all is forgiven.

Kendra is looking forward to her future with Dane, and they have big plans to open a bike and cheese shop. Dane's parents weren't happy at first—they wanted him to make the NHL—

but I think they're warming to the idea of a future filled with all the surprises Dan and Kendra have in story for them.

As for Jesse and me, we're taking it slow. We both have time at college before he goes off to the NHL. He wants me to get a nursing job with the team, because he can't stand the idea of being apart. We still have a couple of years to figure things out. I'm not too worried about it. As long as Jesse is by my side, I know our future will be happy.

I grin, still unable to believe the jersey he gave me for Christmas, or that I'm his number one. My parents and grandparents liked him when I introduced them just last week. But what's not to like? He actually really hit it off with my dad who loves hockey. Who knows, maybe Jesse will bring my family closer.

Christmas music fills the room and I sit back and sip on my hot chocolate. Conversation is lively as everyone rips into their presents, and I just smile and soak it all in.

"Oh look, there's one more under here," Jesse says, and pulls out a big box. He holds it out and my body warms as I take in his mussed hair and low-slung pajama pants. "It's for you, Josie."

I frown. "I already opened my presents."

"You didn't open mine," Jesse informs me.

"Yes, I did. On the boat."

"Can't a guy get his girl two presents?" My heart swells. I love when he calls me his girl. He sets the box on my lap, and the room goes oddly quiet.

"What is it?"

"Open it and see."

I rip into the paper, and open the box, only to discover a smaller box inside. "Nice, Jesse," I say and roll my eyes. I open the next box to find another box, and everyone laughs. I keep this up until I find a very small box, and I'm sure I've reached the end until, once again, there is a smaller box inside. "This better be the end of it," I warn.

Jesse shrugs. "I guess you'll have to open it and see."

I turn my attention back to the box. I open it, and gasp. I lift my head and find Jesse on his knees in front of me. Tears instantly flood my eyes. Is this really happening? Just a few months ago I was nervous and anxious to hang out with Jesse now he's asking me to—.

"Marry me, Josie. Make me the happiest man in the world."

I glance around and take in all the smiles. Never in my life have I felt so loved or cherished. I belong here, with Jesse and his family. I always thought an engagement was a private affair, but Jesse is proposing in front of our loved ones, to show me his family is my family. Just when I thought I couldn't love him more, my heart overflows with everything I feel for him.

"I know it's fast," he begins as I struggle to find my voice. "But I know what I want, and what I want is you, forever." His eyes are full of warmth and love as they move over my face. "I want you to be my wife. I want you to be Josie Campbell, but if you don't want to take my last name, you don't have to. We can do a hyphened name, or you can keep your own name, or I don't know, I can take Carver as mine."

I put my finger to his mouth to stop him from rambling. "I...I want you too, Jesse."

He takes the ring and slides it on my finger. As I admire the gorgeous diamond, he picks up the small box and sets it aside. "That was the end of the boxes," he says softly. "And the beginning of us." He leans in and kisses me as everyone laughs and claps. His head suddenly jerks back. "Wait, you didn't officially say yes."

I laugh. "Yes, Jesse. I will marry you and make you the happiest man in the world."

"Now you get to call me your fiancé and I get to call you my fiancée. That sounds—"

Memories from an old conversation jump to the forefront of my brain and I cut him off and say, "Not so bad."

"Hey," he shoots back laughing.

I playfully roll my eyes as everyone stares at us, not getting the inside joke. "I mean, it could be worse." He pulls me to my feet and wraps his arms around me. I laugh and say, "It sounds amazing, Jesse and any name will do, other than Mrs. Soup..."

HARD BURN

Cathryn Fox

Three years ago:

With exhaustion pulling at me after a long flight from Detroit, where I play college baseball for Michigan State, I step into my best friend's dorm room, glance around and drop my duffle bag onto the floor.

Liam doesn't know I'm back in Nova Scotia, which is why he's not here to greet me. But we've been best friends since we were kids, growing up in the same fishing village in Lunenburg, Nova Scotia. He stayed here in Nova Scotia to play high-level college hockey, and was drafted by Miami. I left to play ball in the States, with the MLB on my mind.

Yawning, I check the time, and it's nearly ten PM. Since I have no idea what time he'll be back to the dorm, I kick off my shoes, strip down to my boxers and climb into his bed. If he's not back in an hour, I'll text him and let him know I'm here. Or maybe he's out with his girl, and I'll simply get a good night's sleep and we'll hang out for the rest of the weekend. That does sound like a better plan.

I close my eyes and roll over, letting sleep pull at me. The next thing I know, the bed dips, and I work to pull myself awake. I'm about to jump up and let Liam know I'm here, but stop when a soft sobbing sound fills the room.

What the hell?

I go perfectly still. Whoever is beside me is crying, and from the soft whimpering sounds, I know it's not Liam. Okay, Josh, get your ass out of his bed and out of this room before the girl beside you—a girl possibly crying over Liam—knows you're here.

I hold my breath, quietly slide out from the covers and put my feet on the floor. Only problem is the old wood floor creaks, and the girl beside me goes completely still. I wait. She waits. A second passes, and her voice finally breaks the quiet.

"Liam?"

The second I hear her soft sweet voice, one that's teased and tormented me over the years, I know it's Ember, Liam's younger sister. A girl I've always had a thing for and could never do anything about. She's completely off limits and no way would I ever break bro-code. I'm not that guy. I take a few deep breaths. How do I handle this? As my brain races— if Liam ever walked In and saw us in bed together, he'd lose his shit—I debate my next move. Except that move is made for me.

The lamp on the nightstand turns on and I cringe as the room brightens. A little gasp of surprise escapes Ember's lips as I sit on the edge of the bed, my bare back to her. I don't want to turn and look. If I catch a glimpse of her between the sheets, possibly naked, everything I've pushed down over the years might come barreling to the surface and demand to be noticed.

"Yeah, it's me," I say quietly.

"What...what are you doing here?"

Don't turn. Don't look.

"I had the weekend off and I was going to surprise Liam."

"He's not here."

"Way to state the obvious." She goes quiet and I grip the bedding and fist it. I don't mean to be an asshole. I really don't. This whole situation is messing with me. "I...should go." I make a move to stand and a hissing sound seeps through my clenched teeth as her small, soft hand lands on mine.

"No, you should stay. I'll go."

Ember is crying.

Unable to help myself I turn in the bed, and my heart clenches as I take in her big, red swollen eyes.

"Hey," I say, and shift, sitting cross legged to face her. "Are you okay?" Of course, she's not okay, dumbass. I glance around Liam's room. She's obviously upset and probably needing comfort from her brother. "What are you doing here?"

She sniffs. "I needed to get out of the sorority." She shakes her head. "I didn't think my first year at Scotia Academy would go down like this."

"First year is always hard." I know for a fact it is. Moving away and finding myself surrounded by strangers is never easy. "Second year will be better." She plucks at the blankets, hurt and...is that shame?...all over her face.

I touch her hand, rubbing my thumb on her wrist, and she takes a fast breath. Her eyes lift, and I'm not exactly sure what's going on, but everything in the way she's looking at me drags my need for her from my darkest corners straight to the tip of my cock.

Run, Josh. Get the fuck out of Liam's room. Now.

She sniffs again, and there is no way in hell I can make a single muscle in my body move. This is my best friend's sister. I care about her, and if she needs someone to talk to, I need to be that guy. I will be that guy.

"Did someone hurt you?" I ask. Yeah, I can be the person to go beat the crap out of some guy if he hurt her. I can deal with anger more than I can deal with the strange heat arcing between us. Then again, maybe I'm the only one feeling it.

"My roommate," she begins, her voice a bit broken. A snort of derision is followed by, "My best friend." Dark lashes briefly close over big, sad blue eyes. "At least, I thought she was my best friend."

Okay, so I don't need to go beat up some dude. Unfortunately. That would have at least let me expel some of the energy coursing through my body like a ninety-mile an hour fast pitch. "I'm sorry," I tell her and shift to put my back against the headboard. She mimics my position, and her thigh rubs up against mine. My arousal spikes and I momentarily curse myself. What the fuck am I doing? No way should I allow her touch to fuck with me like this. Not when she's clearly sad. Am I that much of a selfish bastard?

"She was in bed with my boyfriend. I was out with my study group and came back early."

Okay, I do get to beat some guy up. Things are looking up and I'm not just talking about what's going on in my boxers.

"What's his name and where do I find him?"

She puts her hand on my chest to stop me, and she might as well be giving me a hand job, because yeah, that's where the heat from her fingers has travelled. I grab the blankets and pull them up, hoping to cover my fat cock before she notices it. Judging by the little gasping sound in her throat...I failed.

She swallows. "I don't want you to go."

Is she saying that because she doesn't want me to hurt the guy, or does she have another reason?

Fuck, Josh, don't go down that road.

"I...won't go."

She puts her head on my shoulder, and I instinctively draw her in, and lightly run my fingers through her hair to soothe her. It can't be easy to lose a best friend and a boyfriend all in one night.

"You deserve better than those two."

That sadness reappears and my heart squeezes tight. Tears drip from her cheek and land on my arm. "Does Liam have anything to drink in this place?" I want to help her and have no idea if drinking is the answer. I'm not good at dealing with these kinds of things. Hell, I grew up in a fishing village and a family of guys. At college, I'm surrounded by male teammates, and we don't talk about our feelings. Tenderness is not something that comes naturally to me, I don't think.

"I think he has something in his cabinet." She gestures toward the corner and I ease out of the bed. I find a bottle of vodka and in his fridge discover a soda.

I hold both up. "What do you think?"

"I think it's Friday night and I have a couple of things to drink to. Not good things, but things nonetheless."

She climbs from the bed, and I nearly swallow my tongue as my gaze goes over her matching black bra and panties. As I stare, her cheeks turn red. "Sorry," she apologizes. "I wasn't expecting anyone in Liam's bed."

I try not to sound like I'd just eaten a frog when I respond. "Ah, where is Liam, anyway?"

"He's staying at a friend's tonight. I knew his room was empty, so I came here when I saw my ex best friend and ex-boyfriend shagging."

I have no idea why, but hearing her say shagging hits me and I start laughing.

"You think that's funny?"

I shake my head, and catch the smile forming on her face, and I'm happy I could put it there. "No, it's just...you called it shagging. When did you become British?"

She laughs with me. "It's this book I'm reading. It's a comedy and they talk about shagging. I guess I just have shagging on the brain."

I arch a brow. Do I tell her I have shagging on the brain too? Fuck no. *Get your shit together dude.* "Which book?"

She glances around quickly, an almost panicked look on her face, like I might spot something she doesn't want me to spot. She relaxes. "Oh, it's a book for one of my literature classes," she explains. Why is she lying to me? I'm about to press but she glances at the bottle.

"Are we just going to look at it all night, or are we drinking?"

"Right." I crack the bottle and put a generous amount in two tumblers followed by a bit of soda. I hold my glass out to hers. "What should we drink to?"

She rolls her eyes. "To figuring out who your friends really are."

"Yes, and to a successful second year at Michigan. We won a big college tournament."

She smiles. "I know."

Ah, so she follows me. "Speaking of shagging. Did you know I don't shag during the stretch drive?"

She angles her head, like she's mulling that over, and I shake mine. Why the fuck would I say something like that? Oh, probably because I have sex on the brain. "Drink," I order softly.

I watch her carefully as we clink glasses and we both take a big drink. It burns down the back of my throat, and I'm grateful for something else to feel, other than lust for the woman I'm not allowed to touch.

She cringes and wipes her mouth with the back of her hand, and my throat tightens. I haven't seen her much since I'd gone to the States, and while she was always pretty, I can see that she's become a beautiful woman with a curvy body any man would kill for. What the hell was her ex thinking? Could he not see what was right in front of him? I'm not happy he cheated on her, but I'm glad she found out. She deserves much better. She deserves a guy who'll treat her like the goddess she is.

Goddammit, I want to be that guy.

But I can't.

Tears start flowing again and I take her glass from her, setting it on the counter along with mine. I pull her small, quivering body to mine, and cup her chin, lifting it until our eyes meet.

"I'm really sorry, Embee," I say, using my nickname for her. "Is there anything I can do to make this better? If there is, please tell me and I'll do it."

As Josh holds my gaze, my entire body warms. Honestly, if he knew how I wished I could answer, he probably wouldn't be asking it. This is my brother's best friend, and I know their bro code. Simply put, I'm off limits. I get it, which is why I've always tried to keep my distance from the one guy I always wanted—the guy that's never been interested in me. Josh is a good guy, with a good heart. He and my brother go way back, and even if he was interested, I would never want to come between them.

Right now, though? With my heart a little wobbly after catching my best friend with my boyfriend, I'm a little off kilter, and everything in the way Josh is looking at me, asking what I want...I don't know if I have the strength to keep it to myself anymore.

I realize I'm not model gorgeous like my roommate. In fact, I'm often overlooked. But Josh isn't overlooking me right now. In fact, he's looking at me like I'm everything he's ever wanted.

I put my hands on his shoulders, and he sucks in a breath as his muscles bunch beneath my palms. "Tonight," I whisper quietly, as his hands tighten around my back. He angles his head, his eyes searching my face for answers.

"What about tonight, Em?" he asks quietly.

"Being with you, that would make everything better."

His voice is a soft, agonized whisper when he backs up an inch and murmurs, "Em."

I swallow. God, what am I doing? I don't want him touching me because he feels sorry for me, and clearly, I'm reading him and this situation all wrong. As he stares at me, like he's fighting an internal war with himself, I let my hands fall to my sides, and back up. "I'm sorry. I don't know—"

"Em," he breathes, as he reaches out, snags my hand and pulls me back. My body collides with his, and the second the hardness between his legs hits my stomach, I gasp. His chest rises and falls quickly as his breathing changes, and I put my hands on his chest and go up on my toes.

"Josh..."

His head dips, and his lips find mine for a deep kiss that wraps around my soul and hugs tight. My God, I've been kissed before, but never like this. Then again, none of those guys were Josh, the man I've wanted for as long as I can remember. His big hands go around me, his fingers searing my skin as I move against him, tempting his growing cock with my stomach.

"Fuck, Em," he growls into my mouth, his fingers in my hair. He grabs a fistful and tugs, opening my mouth more so he can taste the depths of me. I moan, having dreamt about this moment for so long. In fact, I wrote about it in my journal.

I'm studying English literature, but my passion is romance writing. I use Josh as my inspiration for every hero I create. People will tell you a fantasy is always better than the real thing. In this situation, they'd be wrong. Kissing Josh in real life is better than all those nights I laid in bed and imagined it.

My fingers race over his body, wanting to touch every inch of him while I can. I'm certain this is a one-night thing, and I damn well plan to take advantage of it. Before I realize what's happening, my feet leave the ground as he picks me up and walks to the bed. He sets me down on the edge and drops to his knees in front of me. His eyes are dark, and full of hunger as they travel to my chest, my black lace bra doing little to hide my arousal.

"Fuck," he murmurs, his hands going to the outer edge of my breasts, a soft caress that pulls a moan from my throat. He lightly touches me, shaping the curves of my body, a delicate exploration, like he's discovering something precious for the very first time. "You are gorgeous." His hands snake around my back and with a quick flick, my bra is falling off my shoulders. Dark eyes lock on my hard nipples and he cups my breasts as he leans into me, taking a bud into his hot mouth.

He moans around my nipple and the vibrations go straight through my body, teasing my arousal to new heights. "That is so good." My words seem to do something to him. With a new sense of urgency about him, like he's totally committing to this night, even though we both know we shouldn't, he lightly scrapes his teeth over my flesh until pain mingles with pleasure. "God, Josh."

Thick fingers dig into my thighs as he widens them even more, situating his big, hard body between my spread legs. My sex moistens as his hands slide up, and I'm pretty sure I no longer know how to breathe as he dips his fingers into my panties, his thumb seeking my throbbing clit. I moan and throw my head back as he rubs it with deft precision, and I move against him, rocking my body to let him know how much I love it.

His head lifts and his eyes meet mine, checking in with me. I move, letting him know I want this and more. I cup his face, and bring his lips to mine for a kiss as he slides a finger into me. The room is dim, with only the lamp on, but it gives sufficient light to views his body. I normally like sex with the lights out. I'm not all that comfortable in my skin. Tonight, however, as Josh tears his lips from mine and bends to press his mouth to my pussy, I feel like a prized possession.

He nips at my panties, tugging them from my wet sex. He breathes in the scent of my arousal and moans hungrily. I move and shift, and work to telegraph a message with my eyes: get me naked already.

He grins up at me, as though understanding, and I press my hands to the bed to lift my hips. His grin widens, as if to tell me how thoughtful I am to help a guy out and I chuckle slightly. My God, this is Josh I'm getting naked for. Never in a million years did I think this would happen.

He drags my panties down my legs, the rough pads of his fingers scorching my skin as they trail along my inner thighs. I stare at his perfect mouth, my eyes pleading with him, desperate to feel it between my legs and he quickly answers my pleas, and nuzzles in. His tongue slides across my sex and I grab fistfuls of his hair, pushing him harder against me. He presses his nose against my clit to apply pressure, and small pulses begin deep in my core.

"Josh," I whisper, simply wanting to say his name as he pleasures me with his mouth. He growls something indiscernible, and licks me from bottom to top and back down again. One thick finger dips back into me and he does a quick check in as small spasms ripple around his finger.

"Em," he groans. "So hot and wet for me."

The key words...for me. I'm pretty sure I've never been this hot, wet or turned on by any other man in the world. If I had it my way, this wouldn't be a one-night thing. It'd be an every night thing. We have my brother to consider, though. He wouldn't like this one little bit.

Hey, you're a big girl, Ember. You can sleep with anyone you want.

While that's true, my brother wouldn't see it that way.

Damn well make Liam see it that way.

Okay, yes, yes, I will. Providing Josh wants more after tonight. If it's as good for him as it is for me, then he's going to want more than one night. Which means I am going to blow his... mind. Somehow. It's not like I'm that experienced. With Josh, though, I want to go all in. I feel less self-conscious and giving pleasure is as important as being pleasured.

He adds a second finger, and vibrations begin deep in my core. Sharp teeth nip at my clit, and then he sucks it in until it's so swollen and stimulated, y brain is no longer able to keep focus.

"Yes," is all I can manage to get out as I grab the back of his head and drag it harder against my pussy. Who am I? I'm not sure, but like I said, I'm a different person with Josh. A freer one, and I like it. My entire body breaks, a dam letting go, and I come all over his mouth and fingers, my hot release pulling a moan from the depths of his lungs. He likes this. He likes my cum on his face. Well, dammit, he can have it there any time he likes.

"Em, baby, look at you."

I meet his hungry gaze, the heat and need in his eyes teasing my arousal again. His face is wet from my release and weirdly, something about that creates a deeper intimacy between us. We've always been friends. Not like this, though. Something is happening here. I'm sure of it.

It could be post-orgasmic bliss, Em.

It could be, and I'm not going to think about that. Not when he has a raging hard-on and I have a free mouth. I move forward, nudging him with my body and he rocks backward. His eyes are dazed, like pleasuring me and making me come has affected him more than me.

I slide off the bed and put my arms around him. He angles his head, still dazed. I reach between our bodies and he groans, throwing his head back as I dip my hands into his boxers and massage his thick cock.

"Em, that is good."

"I want you in my mouth," I whisper and his eyes pop open.

"Yeah?"

His response brings a smile to my face. Why does that seem like such a ludicrous idea to him?

"You don't have—"

"I know I don't have to. I want to." I slide my tongue over my bottom lip to entice him and as his entire body weakens, I nudge him back until he's spread flat out on the floor.

He goes up on his elbows and I position myself between his legs. "Fuck me."

"Yeah, Josh. That's what I'm going to do."

I don't particularly think I'm the blow-job queen, but as I take him into my mouth, deeper than I'd ever taken my boyfriend, he grunts his approval and it fills me with confidence. I shut my eyes, enjoying the flavor on the tip of his cock, and the way he stretches my mouth. This time, I'm not going to think about my performance, hoping I'm doing it right. I'm going to let nature guide me, do what feels right, instead of worrying about whether I'm doing it porn style or not—something my ex watched and wanted me to live up to. Douche bag. Maybe it was a good thing I caught him with my roommate. Honestly, he always judged my performance and up until now, I didn't know that doing what felt right was the key to great sex. Being with Josh is definitely making me see things clearly.

I take him so deep, I cut off my air. I don't care. His groans and grunts of pleasure are all I need to survive.

"Babe," he murmurs. "You're killing me."

I love that. I love that he's encouraging me instead of critiquing me. It turns me on even more and I cup his balls and give them a gentle massage. He thickens even more, and starts panting hard and I prepare for him to burst inside my mouth.

Instead, he pushes on my shoulders, dragging me off him, and the intensity about him is exciting. Each move is filled with purpose as he stands, pulling me up with him. He lifts me easily and sets me on the bed. I back up and watch, transfixed as he strips completely and pulls a condom from his duffle bag. I guess he came home prepared. Was he prepared for me? Lord knows I dreamt about this, but nothing could have prepared me for the real thing.

He sheathes himself and I let my gaze rake over his rock-hard body, muscles built from hard work in the fishing industry, not a gym. He climbs on the bed, a predator about to take down his prey and a shiver races through me from the top of my head to the tips of my toes.

I am so ready for this.

"Babe," he murmurs, and leans over me. I spread my legs and look into his questioning eyes. He knows it, just like I know it, that we're crossing a line we can't come back from.

I race my fingers through his hair. "I want you. I want this. I have for a long time," I say honestly.

His face softens, and he opens his mouth like he wants to say something. I wait and when no words come, I lift and press my mouth to his. His kisses are soft at first, then they turn hungry, and as soon as I wrap my legs around his back, he positions his cock at my entrance and slides into me. Our groans mingle and I close my eyes against the pleasure, wanting to savor this perfect moment. My life has never been better.

The truth is, I wasn't in love with my boyfriend. I'm not sure I can love anyone but Josh. It was the betrayal from my now ex, and my now ex best friend that hurt the most, and knowing I'm just not as appealing as the other women on campus.

Right now, I don't want to think about that. No, I want to think about how we're moving together, instinctively knowing each other's bodies. We touch, taste, give and take, and each time he slides into me, I lose a little more of myself in him. I'm so close, but I want to hang on. I don't want this moment to end. Josh shifts his body, his pelvis pressing hard against my clit with each powered move, and I claw at his back and let go.

He growls into my ear as my cum scorches him through the condom, and he cups my cheeks, drives into me once, and then twice, and throws his head back as he pulses inside me. I moan and revel in each glorious vibration, loving that I could give him this kind of pleasure.

"Josh, I feel you." Panting, his lips fall over mine, and he kisses me with a tenderness that wraps around my soul and hugs tight.

I am in love with this man. I always have been and I always will be.

He collapses on top of me, pressing me down with his body and he quivers as I lightly trail my fingers over his back. This intimacy, it's the best thing I've ever felt in my entire life. I could stay in Josh's arms forever.

He lifts his head, and a warm smile tugs at the corners of his mouth. "Hey," he whispers.

"Hey yourself."

"That was—"

The bedroom door flings open, and both Josh and I stiffen at the sight of Liam. He stands still, confusion on his face as his gaze goes between the two of us. Suddenly, the confusion clears and anger moves in to take its place.

His eyes harden, the muscles in his jaw clench. He starts breathing faster, his fingers balling into fists. "What the fuck?" he hollers.

Josh quickly rolls off me, covering me with the bedding before grabbing his boxers and pulling them on. Liam glares at him. "Liam, it's not what you think?"

I stare at Liam. It's exactly what he thinks. His best friend and his grown-up sister who can sleep with whoever she wants, just had incredible sex.

"Liam," I begin. I don't want him to be upset by this, and he shouldn't be. Wouldn't he want me with someone he loved, someone as great as Josh? Then again, I'm probably getting ahead of myself. Was this just one night of sex for him? Was he promising a future, or was I simply crazy for even thinking we might have one?

"Oh, and what do I think?" Liam asks Josh, completely ignoring me.

"It...it was a mistake," Josh says, his head low.

My gaze jerks to his as he literally pierces my heart with his words. How could he think this was a mistake? I glare at him, wanting him to stand up to my brother, to tell him I'm so much more than a mistake to him. Maybe I'm not, though. Maybe I'm a foolish little girl for thinking Josh could fall for someone like me. Yes, everything in his touch felt real, and true and whispered promises of a future. If that was true, though, he would have spoken up.

Liam takes a threatening step closer. "The mistake was me trusting you."

Josh rakes a shaky hand through his hair. "Liam—"

Liam stalks closer into the room, and points at the gaping door. "Get the fuck out, Josh. I never want to see you again."

JOSH

P resent Day:

With my duffle bag over my shoulder, I walk past the outdoor pool as the Texas sun sets in the distance. My gaze races over the lounge chairs, and while there are a ton of gorgeous girls all dressed in bikinis here at the Vivaldi hotel in Houston, my stomach is too knotted up to appreciate the beauty. How could I not be a hot bundle of nerves? This is game six in the series playoff, with only two wins against Houston Howlers, and I need to perform. All my focus has to be on fitness, rest and tomorrow's game, which means no sex for me. Actually, I never had sex during the college series playoffs. Call me superstitious, but I've carried that tradition into the MLB, playing for Philadelphia Flashers.

Over in the corner of the pool, I spot a group of girls giggling and flirting with some guy. I look closer, and I'm sure he's famous, a movie star, or a rock star, I think.

All I want to do is get to my room, have a protein shake and get some rest. Someone calls my name and I turn. Only problem is, my big bag smacks into someone and the next thing I hear is a yelp and a splash.

Oh, shit.

I drop my bag, and even though I'm dressed in shorts and a T-shirt, I kick off my sneakers and jump into the pool to fish out...Ember?

Big blue eyes stare up at me as I wrap my arms around her to lift her from the water. She gasps and wipes her hair from her eyes, staring at me like she's seeing a ghost from her past, and when it comes right down to it, she is.

Since that night in her brother's room, when he kicked me out of his life, I lost all contact with Ember. My gut clenches just thinking about it, and to this day, there's a big cavern in the center of my chest. How could I have slept with my best friend's sister? It's all my fault, and I don't deserve to have Liam's friendship.

"Embee," I ask. "Are you okay?"

"Josh?" Her confused gaze races over my face as she stares up at me. "Is it really you?"

"It's me," I answer quietly, and glance around as I carry her to the edge of the pool. "What are you doing here?" Houston Texas is a long way from Nova Scotia, and how can she be on vacation? She's fourth year at the academy and classes are in session.

"I...ah...what are you doing here?"

"I'm here for the series playoffs, with the Flashers. We're the away team, staying at this hotel." She blinks up at me, and I get the feeling she knew that. "Is that why you're here?"

She snorts out a laugh. "No," she shoots back quickly and definitively, and my heart sinks a little. Yeah, why after all these years would she even want to see me? The hurt look on her face after I told her brother I'd made a mistake still haunts me. In a way, it was a mistake, but Jesus, I wanted her. I still do. If only I had talked to Liam, told him how I felt and that I wanted more than one night with her, things might have turned out different. Hindsight really is a wonderful thing.

"What are you doing here?" I ask again and her body tightens. I suppose I should set her down at some point.

"I...uh...it's for one of my college classes." Her gaze darts around the pool. "There's a conference, and I'm working on a thesis."

I want to press, and ask for more information, but really, it's none of my business. She coughs, and I set her on the edge of the pool. "Are you sure you're okay?" The sun goes behind a cloud, and she shivers. Maybe she's cold or maybe she's still in shock.

"I'm going to my room. It's getting late anyway."

"I'll take you."

Her body stiffens. "I'm capable of taking myself." There's a hardness in her voice now. I guess she must be thinking back to the last time we saw one another.

She stands, and I nearly swallow my tongue as I take in her body, covered in a small bikini. If I thought she was beautiful three years ago, it's nothing compared to now. She's stunning.

A woman like Ember, she has to have a boyfriend. Not that it matters to me. I could never be with her. After fucking her in her brother's room, breaking the bro-code, and hurting her, I don't deserve more.

"Are you here alone?" She stares at me, like she's not sure how to answer. "Do you have a girlfriend or boyfriend I can call to walk you back to your room?" Subtle, Josh, real subtle.

"I'm here alone. Like I said, it's for research."

She walks over to a lounge chair, picks up a light dress and pulls it on over her bathing suit. She reaches for her big beach bag and I take it from her. "Come on." Giving her little choice, I grab my things, put my hand on her back and guide her inside the hotel. "Which floor?"

"Fourth."

"You're sleeping under me." Her gaze jerks to mine. "I mean, I'm on the fifth floor."

She nods and goes quiet, staring at the elevator button after I press it. "How's your final year going?" I ask.

"Good."

"Do you know what you're going to do after graduation?"

"I'm not sure yet," she answers.

"You used to always talk about being a journalist, or even a teacher."

"Yeah, I'll probably pick one of those things."

Wow, I don't think her voice could lack any more enthusiasm if she tried. "How is...Liam?" I swallow against a tight throat.

"He's playing for Miami."

I nod, knowing that. I've followed his career and I was so happy for him when he went to play for Miami. I debated phoning him for house when he made the team, wanting to call and congratulate him. In the end, I chickened out. He doesn't want to hear from me, and I don't deserve his friendship.

"You should call him," she suggests.

I snort. "You were there..." Shit, I shouldn't have said that. I don't want her thinking about how cruel I was to her. "He kicked me out of his room and his life."

She goes deathly quiet as the doors ping open and we step inside. "And out of mine too, I guess."

Her voice is a low, barely audible whisper, but her words are sharp enough to cut into my hollowed-out chest.

The elevator moves, and my hand brushes hers. "I didn't think you'd want to see me or hear from me again either, Em."

"Yeah," is all she answers.

Did she want to hear from me?

I want to ask, but digging up the past is fucking painful for both of us. What's done is done. We can't change that now, and how could I have called her? I'd made enough of a mess of her and her brother life as it was.

"Do you get home often?" she asks.

"Not as much as I used to when I was in college. Pretty busy on the road. Once the season is over, I plan to head back home for a while." The elevator doors ping open, and I instinctively put my hand on her back to guide her off. Her entire body stiffens under my touch. "Sorry."

"It's okay." She steps off the elevator and walks ahead of me to her room. She swipes the key band on her wrist over the door lock and it pings green. "Thanks for walking me." She holds her hand out and I stare at it for a second. Is she inviting me in? Do I want her to invite me in? Fuck yeah, I do, but crossing the threshold would be the second worst mistake I've ever made. I've hurt her enough. "My bag."

"Oh, right." I slide her bag off my shoulder and hand it over. She takes it from me, and I can't tell if the sound she just made when our hands touched was from hate or desire. Probably hate. She puts her fingers on the door and I stand there, not wanting to stay, but not wanting to leave either. I shift from one foot to the next.

"I hope you win," she says quietly.

"Do you have time to take in the game?"

"I wouldn't be able to get tickets this late." She glances at something on her desk inside the room. "I'm here to work, anyway."

"Okay, I hope you have a great weekend." I put my hand on the doorframe and push off. "See you around, Em." She tucks a wet strand of hair behind her ear. "You look uh...great. Really great actually, and I'm sorry I knocked you into the pool."

"It's okay." She glances down at her wet dress before her eyes turn to me, running down the length of my body. "You look great too, Josh. The MLB has been good for you."

"Been working on fitness and stamina," I say for lack of anything else.

She nods, and looks away as she whispers, "You always had that."

I walk down the hall and listen for her door to click shut. It doesn't and it takes every ounce of restraint I have not to turn around. I head to the stairs instead of the elevator, needing to burn off a bit of pent-up energy and take the steps two at a time. I make a beeline to my room, toss my bag onto the floor and collapse on the bed.

What the fuck just happened?

Oh, you just ran into—literally—the only girl you've ever loved, the only girl you can never have.

I take a few deep breaths and put my forearm over my eyes, wanting to block out painful memories from the past. Too bad they're imprinted on my brain, a constant reminder that I'm not a good guy, and probably don't deserve to play second base for Philadelphia. I'm supposed to meet the team for dinner in an hour and all I want to do is curl into a ball and fall asleep. That way I can forget about the past for a little while. Although every now and then it seeps into my dreams too.

Stomach tight, I sit up and pull my phone from my bag. I scan through my contacts and come to Liam's number. I run my fingers over the screen, and debate on sending him a message. What would I say: Oh, just ran into Ember. Remember when you caught me fucking her?

Groaning, I toss my phone onto my bed and glance around the empty room. Last I heard from my folks, Liam had a girl-friend he was serious about. I snort out a laugh that has no humor. We always used to talk about being each other's best man if we ever got married. Fuck, it's been three years since we talked, and I miss him like crazy.

I miss Ember too.

I grab my phone again and find her contact. I squeeze my fingers around the phone and debate on sending her a message to apologize again, which is just an excuse to begin a conversation. I'm sure she's changed her number too.

Honestly, it seems weird that she's here in Houston for a course at the academy. I wanted to ask more and maybe if I run into her again I will. Seriously, though, what literature course requires her to go to Houston? I can't help but think she was being a bit cagey. What she does and why she's here is none of my business, even though for a second there I thought she might have come to watch the series playoffs.

I glance around the room again and a bout of loneliness hits harder than a fast ball. A lot of the guys on the team are happily married, and while I want the same, how can it happen for me? The one woman I want I can't have. Jesus. I can't sit staring at these four walls any longer feeling sorry for myself. I made my bed when I slept with Ember in her brother's bed, and now I have to lie in it.

Pushing to my feet, I head to the door. Maybe some fresh air will help clear my head. I take the stairs to the main lobby, and that's when I notice all the signs, indicating that there's a romance conference going on at the hotel. Is this what brought her here? Is she doing a thesis on romance writing? Is that something she doesn't want me to know about. I mean, I don't read romance, but I certainly respect the genre, and the work that goes into writing a book. Does Em want to be a writer?

I walk through the hotel and find the guys inside the lobby restaurant. I make my way in, and push those old painful memories to the back of my mind. I don't want the guys to think I'm off my game. Tomorrow is the sixth game in the championship series, a must win game for us, and as a rookie, I need to be at my very best.

I drop down into a chair, and put on my best smile and for the next couple hours the guys and I chat about the game and life. A few of them leave early as they have their families with them. Since I don't have anyone waiting for me, I have no reason to rush off.

It's dark by the time I excuse myself and go to my room to grab my workout gear. Maybe a light workout will help settle my nerves and put me to sleep. I head to the gym and go to the locker room. I tug off my shirt and change into a T-shirt and my workout shorts when my phone pings. I reach for it and nearly swallow my tongue as I read the one word on the screen. One word that sets my heart racing and my legs moving.

15

EMBER

I can't believe how nice everyone is. As an unpublished newbie, it's intimidating to walk into a room full of professional romance writers. I'd been nervous about attending ever since signing up. Apparently, I had no reason to be. A very established author took one look at me and instantly took me under her wing, introducing me to her friends and even her editor.

I yawn, and Susan, my new friend—I totally did a fan girl moment when we met—nudges me. "You're not going to bed yet, Ember. I'm getting us another round."

I try not to appear as tired as I feel. It was a long flight this morning, and I truly don't want to go to bed. I want to soak in every moment of this and learn all I can learn. It's true, I didn't really tell Josh why I was here. My parents think writing is a pipe dream and are guiding me toward teaching. Heck, they don't even know I'm here. This is what I want to do, though. The longer I sit at this table of talented women, the more convinced I am that I can turn my hobby into a career. I'm sure Josh would also think it's impractical, much like my parents—who own a multimillion-dollar fishing conglomerate.

"So, who was that hot guy who knocked you into the pool?" Jessica asks, and I instantly flush. Her eyes go wide. "Do you know him?"

I nod, and take a sip of wine. "He used to be a friend of my brother's. He's here for the series playoffs. Away team."

"Is he single?" Anna, sitting to the right of me asks.

"I think so." I have no idea why the thought of Josh and Anna together gives me a knot in my stomach. Okay, maybe I do. Maybe it's because I never stopped loving him.

"He was like a hero right out of one of our novels," Susan says.

"He's no hero," I whisper under my breath.

Susan angles her head. "What?"

"It's just...we had a thing way back when, and he was my brother's best friend, and now he and my brother don't speak, and I haven't seen him in three years. Running into him today was a huge coincidence, and I don't even believe in coincidences."

Stop rambling, girl.

Susan picks up her wine glass and shakes her head. "Oh, girl, you still have it bad for him."

I'm about to deny it, but why bother. "Yup, I do." I swirl the last drop of wine around in my glass, a new kind of heaviness in my stomach.

"Do you know what room he's in?" Jessica asks.

"No. Even if I did, I wouldn't go. It's over between us."

"Maybe it doesn't have to be," Susan says. "Maybe fate put you both here at the hotel. You two actually seemed like you were pretty close."

I laugh at that. "Yeah, maybe." A long-ago memory hits me. "We actually had a safe word."

All eyes zero in on me and I realize how that sounded. I laugh. "Not that kind of safe word," I explain. "It was a word I could text him, in case I got into trouble, or in a situation I didn't want to be in, or at a party I wanted to escape from. Things like that." I stare at my phone.

"Did you ever use it?" Anna asks.

I nod. "Once back in high school when I was on a date with this guy who was completely obnoxious. I texted Josh the word and he showed up and said there was a family situation and I needed to go with him."

Anna smiles. "That's sweet."

I nod in agreement. "That night we watched chick flicks and ate a bucket of popcorn." I smile at the memory. God, I miss him so much there's a constant ache in my soul. Seeing him today, finding myself in his arms, ripped my already shattered heart into a million smaller pieces. As if sensing my pain, Susan puts her hand on mine.

"Message him."

I give a hard shake of my head. "I can't do that."

"Oh yeah, you can." I'm about to protest, and she says, "I don't think it's over between you two and if it were me, I'd want to rewrite the ending."

"You're a writer," Jessica states. "Send the text and give yourself the ending you want and deserve."

I stare at my phone, my heart racing so hard I'm afraid it's going to crack my ribs. Should I? Oh God, no, I shouldn't. But am I going to do it?

Yeah, I'm going to do it.

I slide my finger across the screen. "He's probably changed his number."

"Okay," Susan says. "If he's changed his number, maybe it's not fate. If he hasn't, maybe it is. You won't know until you try."

Before I can give it any more thought or talk myself out of it, I pull up his contact information and type, "Honeybee." It's funny. We chose that because his family had an apiary on their property, and they always gave our family honey and he used to like to call me Embee. I set my phone on the table and we all stare at it like it might be a bomb ready to go off.

It doesn't.

I sit back when the server comes and brings us all a shot. I pick mine up and hold it up for a salute. "To fate," I toast and we all clink glasses and take our shot. As mine burns down my throat, my phone pings and I choke so hard the alcohol comes out my nose.

"Ohmigod," I yelp, and reach for a napkin.

"Is it him?" my new friends all ask, stretching in their seats to see the screen on my phone, which I might be a little too afraid to touch. What if it is him? Then what? I don't want him to think I'm in trouble and come running. A measure of guilt trickles through me as shaky fingers reach for my phone.

I read the message ten times as everyone waits for me to speak. When I can finally find my voice, I lift my head and take in the anxious stares aimed my way.

"It's him," I gulp out. Everyone starts speaking at once, asking what he said and giving me advice. As soon as the conversation dies down, I explain, "He wants to know where I am."

"Tell him," they shout and I nod, my insides trembling—with nervousness and excitement.

I swipe my fingers across the phone and let him know I'm in the hotel bar. When he responds that he's on his way, I put my phone down and slide my hands over my stomach.

"He's on his way," I whisper quietly, a strange giddiness inside me.

Susan nods, and holds up her wine glass. "It's fate."

I stare at the door, and Anna's hand closes over mine. "Breathe, Ember."

I laugh, and suck in a breath. "What do I say? What do I do?"

"You tell him a bunch of authors were starting to annoy you talking about tropes, and you needed to escape," Jessica suggests.

I groan. "I'm a living, walking, breathing trope, aren't I? In love with my brother's best friend. Or rather ex best friend. God, I'm so pathetic." I honestly hate myself for coming between the two guys, and after Liam kicked Josh out of his room that night I wasn't just hurt by Josh's words, I was also angry at Liam for his behaviour. He's always been overprotective, and I knew I was off limits to his friends, but I straight up told him I was a grown-ass woman and could sleep with whoever I wanted. Granted, sleeping with my brother's best friend in my brother's bed wasn't a smart move. I wish I could go back in time. Would I have slept with Josh? Yes. Would I have done things differently, so my brother didn't walk in on us? Yes. I feel totally responsible for their friendship breaking up, and I know Liam misses Josh terribly. But he can be a stubborn ass.

"It's my favorite trope," Jessica tells me.

"Me too," I admit. "I guess I'm sort of writing mine and Josh's story in my current work in progress. Except I'm also using the revenge trope."

"How does it end?" Susan asks.

I shrug. "I'm having trouble with that. It's why I'm here at the convention. To learn and figure out how to tie it all up." I probably can't bring myself to write the ending, because in real life, mine wasn't a happily ever after.

Susan glances at the door and then back at me. "Now's your chance to write your own ending."

I gulp and my heart jumps into my throat at the sight of Josh storming into the lobby bar, a worried look on his face as he glances around in search of me. I stand, and his gaze locks on mine. A couple of big steps have him standing before me in seconds. He cups my elbow, his gaze roaming over my face and my entire body weakens as he touches me.

He turns to the group of women. "I don't mean to interrupt, but I need to speak with Ember."

"Of course," Susan answers, and I can see her trying to bite back a smirk.

"By all means," Anna pipes in.

Jessica gives a little finger wave. "We'll chat with you tomorrow."

Without words, Josh's hand slides behind my back, and my entire body aches for his touch as he guides me out of the bar and into the wide expanse of lobby. Since it's filled with people—apparently, there's a wedding going on at the hotel too—he walks me out back into the night. The air is warm, as he leads me to the pool, quiet this time of night. Underwater lights create a romantic environment, and the rustling water soothes my ragged nerves.

He looks around, and I can't seem to tear my gaze from his perfect face. "Are you okay?"

"I am," I croak out.

He relaxes. "I was worried, Embee."

Hearing him use my old nickname brings up so many warm, happy memories, and my throat tightens to the point of pain. I miss him so much; tears prick my eyes and I struggle to keep them contained.

I dig my nails into my palms, to get myself together. "I didn't mean to scare you. I just..." *Don't lie, Ember. Tell him the truth.* "I was fangirling all over those romance authors and making a fool of myself. I needed to be rescued."

"You read romance?"

"Yeah, to learn more about the genre."

He angles his head, and he looks like he wants to question me on that. Does he spot my eyes so easily? Okay, it's not really a lie. I am here to learn. The thesis part for a class, maybe that's a little fib.

"I don't know a lot about it. My grandmother used to read one a day. Remember that? It was those spicy ones on the rack, and they had that bright red color."

"I remember," I say with a laugh. "My grandmother read them too. Romance novels have come a long way since those days."

"How so?"

"The heroines are strong, resilient, and don't need rescuing. They fight for what they want, and novelists themselves are smart, savvy entrepreneurs who don't get the respect they deserve."

"Why the hell not?"

"That's a question that I'd need hours to answer."

He nods in understanding. "I'm sorry to hear that. Personally, I have all the respect in the world for them. I know I sure as hell couldn't write a book." He grins. "I can barely string two sentences together."

I laugh. "I remember helping you with your English papers back in high school."

"You're way better at words than I am, Em, and maybe your thesis will help romance novelists get the respect they deserve."

"Thanks," I say, happy to hear him talking like that. For a brief minute, I think about telling him what I'm secretly doing in my spare time. Maybe he wouldn't be as judgemental as my parents.

I open my mouth only to close it again as his head dips and the energy between us shifts, becomes more electric, sexual. "Was escaping those novelists really why you sent me the safe word, Em?" he asks, his voice a soft whisper that flutters around me and teases the truth from me. I stare up at him and get the sense that a fib is not the answer he wants.

"Seeing you today. It's just been so long, and...I miss you." Every muscle in his body stiffens, and that's when I wonder if messaging him was a mistake. "You were probably busy. I'm sorry. I didn't mean to drag you away from whatever it was you were doing."

I back up, ready to run to my room and stay there until the conference is over, just to avoid running into Josh again. "Em," he growls firmly, and snakes his hand out, tugging me to him so hard, I lose my balance in my heels and fall against him, knocking him off balance.

"Shit." He tumbles backward and the next thing I know we both land in the pool with a splash. Again. It breaks the tension between us, and I can't help but laugh.

"Did you do that on purpose?" He asks, slicking his hair back, as he grins at me. "Payback for knocking you in earlier?"

"Are you saying you did it on purpose earlier?"

"It was an accident, Em."

"I'm not so sure about that," I tease, even though I know it was an accident. I'm so not into revenge and maybe that's why I can't quite get the ending to my book right. I would never want to hurt Josh, even if his words gutted me and left me a broken for years. I love him too much for that.

He swipes water from his face. "So, we're even then?"

I splash him, soaking his face again. "Now we're even."

"Hey."

Laughing, I swim away, but he's faster and stronger and reaches me in seconds. He pulls me to him, and losing all common sense, I wrap my arms and legs around his body. All humor fades from his face, and I'm no longer laughing either.

"Josh," I manage to get out as our eyes meet and hold.

"Embee..."

I swallow. "Why am I always wet when I'm around you?" Ohmigod, did I really just say that? "I mean, this is the second time we fell into the pool." I glance down at my soaked dress and tug it away from my breasts. It makes a sucking noise, and the sound is followed by Josh's strangled growl.

"Embee..."

"I...I..." I stare at him, wanting nothing more than to feel his lips on my mouth, on my body, between my legs. I can't tell him any of that. Look what happened last time. "What?" I ask as he continues to stare at me.

"I missed you too."

JOSH

Ember begins to shiver in my arms and I'm not sure if she's cold or reacting to me telling her I missed her. Our past isn't a great one. I lost everyone I loved that day in her brother's room. Maybe going forward, I can change that. I might not be able to mend things with Liam, but I'm beginning to believe I can with her. She told me she missed me and I'm grasping her words tight in my heart, hoping for a fresh start. I want us to build something new—something better. If that's what she wants.

It's true, I don't deserve her. I don't deserve love after the way I treated her brother and hurt her with my callus words. Tonight, though, I can't help but want to grasp this opportunity to start again, to make things right. I don't have sex before a big game. It's a ridiculous superstition, but something I've stuck to none the less. Right now, though, I'm not going to miss this chance with Ember. The game is important to me for sure, the most important one of my career so far. Ember, however, is the most important woman in the world to me, and I need to show her that.

"Let's get you inside and warmed up."

She nods, and brushes water from her bottom lip. Unable to help myself, I bend and press my lips to hers. She moans into my mouth, her sounds telling me she wants this as much as I do, but I need to hear it from her.

"Em," I whisper. "Do you want this?"

"I want this," she says so softly she's hard to hear.

"Back in college—" She puts her finger over my lips, shutting down my apology. I've thought long and hard over the years at how I handled that situation. I did everything wrong.

"The past..." she whispers. "Not right now, Josh. Please."

"Okay." I carry her from the pool and water drips at our feet. Thank God her purse didn't take a swim. I snatch it up and carry her inside. All eyes turn to us, and I keep my head down and walk straight to the elevator. I press her floor and we remain silent, her body shivering in my arms as I carry her to her room, open the door and take her inside.

I set her down by the bed, and she tugs on her dress. "I need to warm up."

"You have two options."

She blinks up at me and I continue with, "You can jump in the shower, or I can strip off your wet clothes and warm you with my hands and mouth."

Her body quakes, and her breathing comes a little faster. "I think I like option two."

"Yeah, me too." I close the distance between us, and walk around her to unzip her dress. She quivers as I slide it down her wet flesh, and let it pool at her feet. I lightly run my fingers up and down her arm to create heat with friction and she moans, her wet hair spilling down her back as her head rolls to the side.

I unhook her sexy bra and toss it before walking around her and sinking to my knees. The sweet scent of her skin, still plays havoc with my body after all these years. It fills my senses as I press my nose to her stomach and breathe her in. Her fingers tangle in my hair as she rocks against me, moving her hips to let me know exactly what she wants. Damn if I don't want to give it all to her.

I grip the lace on her panties and tug them down. She balances on one leg and then the other as I remove them. Once I have her completely naked, I grip her thighs. "Spread for me, Em."

She widens her legs and I part her pretty pink nether lips with my fingers, taking my time to admire the sight of her perfect pussy. She whimpers and rocks and I sigh, wanting to stare at her all night, but she needs other things from me, and the truth is that I also need to do those things to her.

I lean into her, and run my tongue over her hot pussy, and she quivers. "Warming up?" I ask between each delicious lick.

"No," she says, and I laugh. "Still cold. Freezing actually."

"Maybe this will help." I press my face into her pussy and eat at her, sucking, nibbling and tasting the depths of her.

"Yes," she cries out. "Yes, Josh just like that."

Fuck, how many years have I spent wanting to hear my name on her lips? I swear to God, I must be dreaming.

Suddenly, catching me by surprise, her entire body stiffens, and it's not from pleasure. "Em," I ask and glance up. The stricken look on her face nearly stops my heart.

"We can't do this."

I look around, expecting her brother to be standing there. "If you don't want—"

"Oh, I do want. I also remember that you don't have sex before games. You can't break that tradition now, Josh. Not for me."

"I'd never break that rule for anyone but you, Embee," I answer quietly, and go back on my heels as she stands there, her arms across her chest.

"Josh...what if sex interferes with your game?"

Not having sex with her is going to interfere with my life, and I can't let this opportunity to be with her go. "I want you, Em. I want this, tonight, with you."

Her gaze races over my face and my entire body is tight. If she walks away from me, like I did to her in her brother's dorm room, I might die right on the spot and that would definitely interfere with my game. I bite down on the inside of my cheek, hating myself for how I left her three years ago. I was cruel and now I don't deserve this, but her body is beckoning mine, and I need to give her this, to let her know she's desirable, and everything I've ever wanted in a woman.

"I want you too," she answers and steps into me. I heave a sigh of relief and pull her to my body, wrapping my arms around her waist to hold her stomach to my face. Her fingers race through my hair, and she slides to her knees, joining me on the floor. "Why do we always end up on the floor?" she teases, easing the tension between us.

"The bed always seems too far away."

She reaches between our bodies and cradles my cock through my wet workout shorts. "Yeah, definitely too far when you're in this state." She grins and I love the teasing, the easy comradery. It reminds me of old times. She said we can't go back, and I won't, but we sure can go forward.

Her hand dips into my shorts and the second she wraps her small hand around my cock, it thickens even more. She strokes me from base to crown, dipping into my pre-cum and rubbing it around my crown.

"I love the way you touch me," I growl, and slide my hand around the back of her head to bring her beautiful mouth to mine. I kiss her deeply as she strokes me, and as pleasure rips through my body, I slide a finger into her. She moans and rocks into me, as we both give and take with our hands. "Warming up?" I ask.

"Afraid not."

I chuckle into her mouth and she growls as I remove my finger from her tight center. I stand, pulling her up with me and make fast work of my clothes. I'm about to pick her up and lay her beneath me on the bed, only to go completely still as she gazes at the tattoo near my heart. She blinks rapidly, and as though moving of its own accord, her hand snakes out and she lightly traces the bumblebee.

"Josh?" she murmurs quietly, her head lifting, her gaze locking on mine. "This...this bee..."

She blinks at me, confusion and something that looks like hope brimming in her eyes. "I got it, after...you know."

The room is silent, save for the sounds her throat makes as she swallows. "It's our word."

"Yeah."

Her chest rises and falls quickly, and every ounce of love I have for her flares hot inside my body. Needing her in my arms, needing to be inside her, I pick her up and walk backward to the bed. I sit, and she straddles me.

"Like I said, I missed you too." I take a breath as she continues to trace the tattoo and I could fucking sob at the mixture of pain and loss in her eyes. I feel it as intensely as she does. "Getting this, it reminded me of you every day, and reminded me of how badly—"

Before I can finish, her mouth is on mine, kissing me with need. I kiss her back with all the pent-up hunger and years of wanting her, flaring inside me. I hold her tight, so tight I'm not sure she can breathe, and she digs her knees into the mattress and lifts herself up. My cock jumps upright, and she lowers herself onto it, groaning as I fill her. Something niggles in the back of my brain.

"Condom," I finally remember.

She goes still. "I'm clean and I have an IUD."

"I'm clean too, Embee. I've never had sex without a condom, but I want to with you. You feel so fucking good." Sex without a condom, no barriers keeping skin from skin, but also no barrier protecting my heart if we can't move forward and find a future together probably isn't a great idea. Yet, I'm going to do it anyway. I have to do something. I can't keep living life as a shell of my former self. Losing my perfect woman and my best friend, made getting through every day painful, and forcing a smile, keeping my focus on the game, is getting harder and harder.

I hold her hips and pull her down onto my cock, burying every last inch of myself inside her hot, tight sheath. Christ, we'd only done this once, and while I've been with a few girls, none of them had ever compared to Ember, and none ever will. This is home. Where I belong.

"Josh," she murmurs and runs her teeth over my shoulder, grazing my flesh in a way that strokes right to my balls.

My hands go to her back and I spread my fingers, wanting to touch her all over. She presses her breasts against my face, and I take a pert nipple into my mouth, sucking and licking and savoring the sweet taste of her.

I pick her up, lifting her from my cock, only to pull her down again, and her moans of satisfaction race through my body. "Fuck, Em...this is...God, it's so..." She's the writer, the one doing an English degree, so maybe she'll be able to put to words what I'm feeling.

"Transcendent," she answers.

"Yeah, that's it. Transcendent. Perfect. Incomparable." Being with her is unlike anything else in the world. I love her. I've always fucking loved her.

She pushes on my shoulders until I'm flat on the bed, and she takes control of our love making. With her hands on her breasts, she moves her hips, and I swear to God, it's the most beautiful sight I'd ever seen. She rocks her gorgeous hips, and with her pussy spread wide, I put my finger on her swollen clit as my cock disappears inside her, only to reappear each time she goes up on her knees.

My thumb swirls her clit, and she moans, and I love how she reacts to my touch. I want to touch her like this every day, and give her pleasure beyond comparison. "Em," I whisper, needing her name on my tongue. "God, Em, you are beautiful."

"You make me feel beautiful."

She moves faster, a new kind of confidence and determination settles about her as she rides me with wild abandon. I love watching her let go, giving herself over to me and the pleasure my cock brings.

I grip her hips and help lift her, wanting to take the pressure off her legs, and she gyrates as I take over, controlling the depth and rhythm. A little gasp catches in her throat and her lust-imbued gaze races to mine.

"Josh..."

Her words fall off, but I get it. There is so much more going on between us, more than just sex and pleasure.

"I know," I tell her. "I know, Em."

She nods, and I power into her, and her mouth opens and closes as her hot muscles clench around my pistoning cock, gripping and massaging, tormenting all my self-control. A second later, her hot cum pours over my cock, searing me from the inside out, and teasing my arousal to completion.

"Babe," I cry out, and hold her down as I spill my seed high inside her.

"I feel you, Josh." Her muscles milk my release as I come and come some more, until I'm drained and have no idea which way is up or down, or even what my name is.

"Em," I groan as she falls over me, her hard nipples scoring my chest as they scrape against my pounding heart, as it swells with all the love I have for her. I roll, taking her with me, until her body is beneath mine. I kiss her, my cock still deep inside as our tongues lazily tangle. I'm in no hurry to pull out or for this night to end, even though I need to get back to my room and get a good night's sleep before tomorrow's series playoffs game. We're expected at the stadium pretty early.

Her fingers trail over my back and I shiver. "Are you cold?" she teases.

I laugh. "Are you warm?"

"If I said I wasn't, can we do that again?"

I brush her hair from her face, and shift to the side, until my cock slips from her body, and we both groan at the teasing friction. "Yes, we can definitely do that again."

"What time do you have to be back in your room?"

I glance at the clock. "Don't worry about it."

"I want you at the top of your game tomorrow," she tells me as her gaze goes back to the bumblebee. A small smile touches her mouth and my heart wobbles in my chest as she reaches out and lightly traces it, knowing what she means to me, and it's easy to tell how touched she is at the reason behind the tattoo.

I roll back on top of her, my cock getting ready for round two. "The only thing I'm interested in being on top of right now is you."

EMBER

I roll over in my big comfy bed, and as memories from last night invade my tired brain and satiated body, my hand snakes across the sheets to find the other side cold and empty. Disappointment tightens in my chest. Did Josh get up in the middle of the night and go back to his room? He probably did and while I know he's here to win the series playoffs, and rightfully needs his sleep, it doesn't mean I don't miss him.

A strange rustling noise from across my room reaches my ears but doesn't really register for a moment. I roll back over so I can relive every glorious moment with Josh. My body tingles in all the right places and everything in his touch last night, the way he looked at me and talked to me, spoke of a future together.

When that strange noise grows louder, reminding me of papers rustling, I open my eyes and go up on my elbows. My heart jumps into my throat the second I see Josh sitting at the desk, two take-out cups of coffee in a corrugated cardboard tray beside him as he flips through the printed pages of my current manuscript. Ohmigod, he's reading my novel. I try to speak, to say something, but my words get lodged in my throat. I sit up a little straighter and take in his posture. His back muscles are tight, and I can't even imagine what is going through his head as he reads parts of...our story.

I sit all the way up and the bed squeaks. Obviously aware that I'm now awake, his head lifts and his shoulders are practically at his ears as he remains still, like he can't bear to turn around and look at me, which worries the hell out of me. Does he think the entire book is about our past, and our future? In a sense, it is about our past relationship. In the manuscript, however, the heroine is out for sweet revenge.

"Josh," I murmur tentatively and he takes in a fast breath. "It's not what you think." The chair wheels squeal as he slowly turns my way and the pain and sadness in his eyes rips through me. "Josh," I hurry out quickly, and toss the blankets off to go to him.

He holds one hand up, palm out to stop me. "You're writing a romance book?" I nod quickly. "That's why you're here?" His voice is laced with suspicion.

"Yes."

"Really, Em? Or are you here to exact sweet revenge on the guy who hurt you three years ago?"

My throat squeezes tight. "No, Josh."

"No?" He picks up the pages of the manuscript I'd been editing with my red pen. "How can you say no when it's all right here in black, white and red?"

"It's not what you think."

"Yeah, you keep saying that." He rakes a shaky hand through his hair. "What a coincidence that your hero's name is Josh."

"It's just...I guess maybe it's a little about you, about what happened to us years ago."

"Wow," he blurts out. "I guess now I know why you lied and said you were here for your thesis."

"I didn't want to tell you—"

"Right, because if I knew this weekend was about payback and revenge, I would have ruined it for you." The shakiness in his voice reverberates through me and slices into my heart. How can he think I'd do something like this? Does he not know me at all? I try to speak, but my words are stuck in my throat. "If I'd known, I wouldn't have broken my abstinence rule before a series playoffs game and slept with you," he adds. He goes quiet for a long moment, and my mind races. How can I make this right? He snorts. "You knew I was going to be here, didn't you? None of this meeting was a coincidence."

My God, he really thinks I went to such great lengths to get payback.

I throw my legs over the bed, and his gaze drops to my naked body. I quickly scramble to my suitcase and pull out a pair of shorts and T-shirt. He sits in silence as I dress. "Josh, if I can just explain."

"Explain that you were out to hurt me? That you hate me so much you actually had sex with me to keep me from being at the top of my performance in a crucial game?"

My heart sinks into my stomach. "Is that what you think of me?"

He stares at me long and hard. "I'm sorry about the past, Em. I'm so fucking sorry." I glance down and he groans. "I thought this weekend.... I thought I was making it right, and this..." He shakes a few sheets of paper.

"How much did you read?"

"Enough to know what's really going on here."

"No, you don't because you didn't read the ending."

"There was no ending."

"That's because it's not finished. Just like we're not finished." I remember what Susan said: Now it's your chance to write your own ending.

"Of course, it's not finished. You needed to hurt me, and then see how it all plays out before you could write it."

I stand. "It's romance, Josh. Romance stories have happily ever afters. Always."

His brow pulls tight with confusion all over his face, and he wags his finger back and forth between the two of us. "Not this story." He stands. "What we did before, and now..." He stares at the unmade bed. "...was obviously another mistake."

Those old painful words cut twice as deep as last time. I stare at him and try to breathe through the ache in my chest. I love this man. I love him with everything in me, yet he thinks I'm capable of such cruelty. Tears pool in my eyes and instead of running to me and brushing them away like he had that night in my brother's room, he just stands there hovering, battling with his own emotions.

"I didn't tell you I was writing a romance because no one takes it seriously," I explain in a last-ditch effort to show him this isn't what he thinks, and that while a part of the book was about us, a big part was also fiction: a revenge trope. Which was never part of my plan with Josh.

"You didn't think I'd take it seriously or support it?" he asks, the hurt on his face slicing my heart into tiny pieces. "I kind of remember saying I had respect for romance writers."

Okay, I'm not making my situation any better here, or proving I wasn't out for revenge, and I guess in a way I can see why he thinks this is all about him.

He pulls the paper coffee cups from the corrugated cardboard tray and hands one to me. "This is for you. It was nice knowing you, Ember." He turns, and walks out the door. I'd say he was taking my heart with him, but that would be a lie. He's had it with him since he walked away from me three years ago.

The door slams with a bang, and the tears fall down my face until the room blurs around me. My phone pings, a reminder that I have a session in thirty minutes. How can I walk into a room of professionals after having my heart torn from my chest, leaving nothing but a gaping hole? All I want to do is crawl back into my bed and stay there until the weekend is over. I flop down, deciding to do that, and the warm scent of Josh on the pillow has me sitting back up.

God, I can't stay in this room where we made love all night long. Needing an escape, I take a fast shower, washing last night from my skin as I work to get my tears under control. Once done, I put on a pretty dress, grab my laptop and take one last glance at my printed manuscript before walking out the door. It locks behind me and I shake my head.

Why had I left my manuscript on my desk last night?

I guess I never thought I'd be going back to my room with Josh, and I'd been doing some editing earlier. If only I'd had the foresight to tuck it away, and when push comes to shove, there really is a part of me that can see why Josh came to the conclusions he did. It was very coincidental that a romance writers conference and the series playoffs away team were staying at the same hotel, and like Josh said, the proof was all there in black, white and red.

Downstairs, the hotel is bustling with so much going on. I search the crowd for a friendly face, and spot Susan waving me over. I square my shoulders and try to appear put together as I approach. She takes one look at my face, and her eyes soften.

"Oh no, Ember." Like a fool, I start crying and she puts her arm around me and guides me to one of the chairs. "What happened?"

"It was great. Everything was great, until…" I swallow and hiccup, and she waves to Anna to grab us a couple of coffees. "I don't want to keep you from the sessions."

"You're not." She frowns. "Did I give you bad advice?"

I shake my head no. "He read my manuscript…and assumed."

Her eyes go wide. "The revenge plot?"

"Uh huh."

"Oh no."

I nod. "Exactly. Now he thinks—"

"You were out to hurt him."

I nod. "I would never do that, though." I swipe at my wet eyes. "He wouldn't listen to me."

Anna shows up with our coffee and sits next to me. I sip my coffee as Susan explains what happened, and Anna puts her hand on mine. "Make him listen."

"How?"

"Hey," Susan whispers quietly and I meet her concerned and caring gaze. "Would the heroine in your book sit back and do nothing?"

"No."

"Would she use everything in her arsenal and go after what she wanted?"

"Yes."

She leans back. "Okay then, you have your answer."

She's right. I'm going to fight for what I want, and give us the ending we deserved three years ago.

Even though we lost, I played the best game of my life, channeling all my hurt and anger into the game and nearly catching every ball that was hit my way. I'm disappointed we lost, of course, and my insides are still seared raw, but with the loss comes sadness for all the players, so at least I don't have to put on a happy face.

We make our way into the locker room, and we're talking quietly, disappointment heavy in the air, but we all played a fantastic sixth game, and I think, despite everything that went down with Ember, I proved myself to these guys.

"Hey, Josh," Kalen Bateman, the pitcher, and the guy that took me under his wing when I joined the team, says as he pats me on the back. "Great game."

"Thanks," I say to the man who is the father figure to the younger players. "You too."

"We'll get 'em next year," he tells me and I love his positive attitude.

"Damn right we will."

We go to our lockers and I strip off and jump in the shower. All I want to do is hop on a plane and go back home, but tonight the guys will all want to get together back at the hotel for a drink and I pray I don't run into Ember.

After we're all showered, we get on the bus and head back, and we're all mostly quiet. Some guys are playing games on their phones, some are talking to their loved ones, and others are just resting. I stare at my phone. It's been a long time since I had anyone I could call and talk to. Fuck man, I miss Liam. I used to call him and tell him everything. I still think of him when something good or bad happens. Liam was my confidant, and maybe if I'd told him how I felt about his sister, and explained I wasn't looking for a fast hook-up, things might have turned out differently.

I guess it's too late for that now.

The bus pulls up to the hotel and we all pile off, agreeing to meet for a drink after we drop our things off. I head to my room, and debate on whether to go down to the lobby bar or not. Maybe a couple of strong drinks will help me forget what a shit show my life is right now.

My phone pings and I snatch it up. While Ember hurt me, I still hope it's her. It's not. It's Kalen wondering where the hell I am. Maybe they have something planned for the rookie.

I make my way down and put on a smile as the romance novelists Ember was with ask if they can take pictures with me. I oblige and after a round of selfies, I head to the lobby bar. I find myself scanning the room, looking for Ember. Kalen puts his hand up and waves me over.

"Hey," I say as I drop down into a chair and he slides a beer in front of me. I can't help but glance around again.

"She's not here?" he asks.

"What?" I turn back to him and notice the way his eyes have narrowed in on me.

"The girl you're looking for, she's not here." I open my mouth about to protest, when he says, "Don't shit me, buddy. We're a team, here for each other, so out with it."

I exhale and sit back in my chair as I tell him all about Liam and Ember and what went three years ago and earlier today. "Wow, she sounds like a total bitch," he snaps, "You're better off without her or Liam in your life."

"No," I say quickly. "She's not a bitch, and Liam was just reacting. I handled it badly back in college."

"Fine, Liam was reacting, but this Ember chick, what a piece of work." He snorts and shakes his head. "You dodged a bullet, my friend."

He takes a long drink as he stares at me, like he's gauging my reaction. "Don't say that. She's really sweet." My heart thumps with pain as I ache for her.

He sets his beer down. "If she was sweet, then why would she be out for revenge?"

"I...I don't know." Am I handling all this badly again? Accusing her of something that's not true, reacting, like Liam reacted all those years ago?

"You must be wrong about her being sweet," he says.

"No, I'm not. She's sweet and kind and funny, and..." God, when I touch her, when she touches me, it feels so right. I run shaky fingers through my hair, as my mind goes back to last night, and all the nights before I hurt her. Ember was always there for me, just like I was always there for her.

"The story, this revenge plot, was about you, wasn't it?" Kalen asks.

"Yeah, she said it was. Parts of it anyway." I pause, as her words ping around in my brain. I'm not a novelist, so I don't really know much about putting a book together. "She said something about the ending. It wasn't finished."

He snorts out a laugh, much like I did when she mentioned the ending. "Yeah, she couldn't write it because she needed to see how it played out."

My throat squeezes tight. "That's exactly what I said."

"Right, so it's settled. You're better off without her."

I take a big drink of my beer and glance around again. "Why does the thought of never seeing her again gut me?"

"Because you love her."

"I do love her," I admit.

He shrugs. "But she's a bitch, so forget about her."

"No, she's not, and it's not that easy." I shoot back, anger racing through me as I defend her once again. He grins at me. "What?"

"You keep defending her, Josh."

Ah, okay, I get it. He was pushing me, to see how I'd react, and to get me thinking. "Yeah," is all I can push past my tight throat.

"Is there some part of you, that college kid that lost so much and is afraid to try and then lose again? That college kids who hopes she wasn't out for revenge, and you read it wrong, because you're afraid?"

I square my shoulders. "I know what I read."

He leans into me, seeming fatherly. "What about what you didn't read?" I stare at him not understanding. "The ending, you didn't read that," he explains.

"It wasn't written."

"If you had to write the ending, what would you write?" I open my mouth and close it as he grabs a napkin and slides it across the table to me. I stare at it, as he calls the server over and borrows a pen. "Write it," he suggests. "Put it down on paper."

As my heart thumps, I shake my head. "I'm not a writer, and..." As I protest, I grab the pen and quickly scribble my version of the ending on the napkin. I set the pen down and my phone pings. I grab it, and my heart jumps into my throat as I read "Honeybee."

"It's her."

Kalen gestures toward the door. "You'd better go."

I quickly text back, asking where she is, and the second she answers, I'm on my feet. I reach her room in record time and she answers on the first knock. The mere sight of her standing before me in a silk robe nearly makes me sob. I love her so fucking much and can't imagine another three years, let alone a lifetime, without her.

"Ember," I murmur, my voice low, tortured and breathless. "Are you okay?

"Not really. Are you?" I shake my head and she begins, "I know you don't want to see me, and you might never want to talk to me again." She hands me a couple of sheets of paper. "But you need to read this. I spent the evening writing it."

"What is it?"

"The ending I want for us." She opens the door wider and gestures to the desk chair. I step inside and she touches my arm. I turn to her. "I'm sorry about the championship, Josh." I nod and drop into a chair.

"Ember," I whisper as I read her happily ever after, and a few jokes in there about her being the consolation prize to the series playoffs.

Really, she thinks she's a consolation prize?

I stand, and shake my head hard as my heart pounds. "This is wrong. You have it all wrong, Ember."

Her face pales, and she backs up an inch, dropping onto the corner of the bed. "I thought it was a great ending. I thought you could see that I'm not...that I wasn't..."

"I know what you are and what you're not." She stares at me in confusion as I take my phone from my pocket, search my contacts and hit dial. The phone rings, and my eyes are locked on Ember's as she stares at me, her expression perplexed. The phone rings three times, and I try to quiet my racing heart as Liam picks up.

"Hey," he says quietly that one word so steeped in pain and loss I know he's been hurting as much as I have for the last three years.

"Liam," I say, and Ember's eyes go wide.

"Josh," she whispers, and puts her hand on my leg. "What are you doing?"

I cover the phone. "What I should have done three years ago."

"Liam," I begin. "I'm in love with Ember. I've been in love with her for as long as I can remember. I shouldn't have slept with her that night without telling you how I felt first. I knew she was off limits, but what you need to know is what happened between us wasn't a random hook-up. I'd never do that to her or to you. I handled it all badly, and what we did wasn't a mistake. I never, ever should have said that. The mistake part was not telling you how I felt about her. I love her and want to spend the rest of my life with her." Silence lasts for so long, I begin to worry that he hung up on me. "Liam?"

"I'm the one who made the mistake," he says quietly, and I exhale loudly as a sob catches in my throat. "I'm sorry, Josh. I reacted. I mean just seeing you two…"

"I get it, bud. Believe me I do. None of it went down right and I'm so fucking sorry."

"I'm fucking sorry, too."

I hold Ember's gaze. "Ember is with me now. We ran into each other in Houston."

"What's she doing in Houston?"

"I'll let her explain that to you when she sees you. I just need you to know I love her and I'm going to spend the rest of my life being everything she needs. If that's what she wants."

I wipe away a tear from her face, and my heart pounds with everything I feel for her.

Liam's voice is shaky when he says, "I've had three long years to think about this, Josh, and there isn't any other guy I'd want her with."

"We okay, Liam?" I ask.

"Yeah, we're okay."

"Let's make plans to get together soon."

"Those are the best words I've heard in a long time."

"When Ember and I get married, will you be my best man?"

Ember starts crying as Liam says, "Okay, I was wrong. Those are the best words I've ever heard. Go be with Ember. We'll talk later, man."

I end the call, drop to one knee in front of Ember, and take her hand. "I know this is fast, Embee," I begin, even though it's not. I've loved her forever. "But will you marry me?" She goes quiet, and I stare at her, search her face. "Ember?"

"Josh," she begins. "All this...the game, the loss, the...are you sure this is what you want? Are you just reacting...all the emotions of the day?"

I pull the napkin from my pocket, making a mental note to thank Kalen for making me put words to paper. She takes the napkin and her eyes fill with tears as she reads: *Marry me.* "I wrote it before you messaged me. It's how I wanted things to end, or rather begin."

"Yes," she answers softly. "I'll marry you." I put my arms around her and kiss her with all the love inside me. I break the kiss and she frowns. "Wait. I don't understand. You said I had it all wrong. What exactly did you mean?"

"You're not the consolation prize, Ember. You are the grand prize, the home run, and having you as my wife makes me the ultimate winner."

She grins and pushes me until I fall back on my heels. She stands and unties her robe. "Oh, so you're saying you don't want the consolation prize I have for you under here?" She widens her robe, teasing me with her lush cleavage.

I glance up at her, the happiest man in the world. "Well, when you put it that way."

Her smile widens as she opens her robe. "Why don't you get over here and let's talk about that home run."

"Yeah, home run," I say, my brain shutting down as it loses blood. "But first I need to touch each base, slowly, and carefully with my hands and my tongue." Her moan of pleasure puts the pieces of my heart back together, and while we lost the championship today, with Ember and Liam back in my life, I truly am the winner.

———

Thank you so much for reading books 10-12 in my Scotia Storm Series. I hope you loved them as much as I loved writing them. If you haven't read the rest in the series, information can be found here! https://amzn.to/3PoCNrD Or here: https://cathrynfox.com/series/scotia-storms/

ALSO BY CATHRYN FOX

Scotia Storms

Away Game (Rebels)

Warm Up (Rebels)

Crash Course (Rebels)

Home Advantage (Rebels)

Shut Out (Rebels)

Moving Target (Rivals)

Face Off (Rivals)

Scoring Fast (Rivals)

Opposing Teams (Rivals)

Deal Breaker (Rebels)

Hard Burn (Rivals)

Fake Out (Rivals)

End Zone

Fair Play

Enemy Down

Keeping Score

Trading Up

All In

Blue Bay Crew

Demolished

Leveled

Hammered

Single Dad

Single Dad Next Door

Single Dad on Tap

Single Dad Burning Up

Players on Ice

The Playmaker

The Stick Handler

The Body Checker

The Hard Hitter

The Risk Taker

The Wing Man

The Puck Charmer

The Troublemaker

The Rule Breaker

The Rookie

The Sweet Talker

The Heart Breaker

In the Line of Duty

His Obsession Next Door

His Strings to Pull

His Trouble in Talulah

His Taste of Temptation

His Moment to Steal

His Best Friend's Girl

His Reason to Stay

Confessions

Confessions of a Bad Boy Professor

Confessions of a Bad Boy Officer

Confessions of a Bad Boy Fighter

Confessions of a Bad Boy Doctor

Confessions of a Bad Boy Gamer

Confessions of a Bad Boy Millionaire

Confessions of a Bad Boy Santa

Confessions of a Bad Boy CEO

Hands On

Hands On

Body Contact

Full Exposure

Dossier

Private Reserve

House Rules

Under Pressure

Big Catch

Brazilian Fantasy

Improper Proposal

Boys of Beachville

Good at Being Bad

Igniting the Bad Boy

Bad Girl Therapy

Stone Cliff Series:

Crashing Down

Wasted Summer

Love Lessons

Wrapped Up

Eternal Pleasure Series

Instinctive

Impulsive

Indulgent

Sun Stroked Series

Seaside Seduction

Deep Desire

Private Pleasure

Captured and Claimed Series:

Yours to Take

Yours to Teach

Yours to Keep

Firefighter Heat Series

Fever

Siren

Flash Fire

Playing For Keeps Series

Slow Ride

Wild Ride

Sweet Ride

Breaking the Rules:

Hold Me Down Hard

Pin Me Up Proper

Tie Me Down Tight

Stand Alone Title:

Hands on with the CEO

Torn Between Two Brothers

Holiday Spirit

Unleashed

Knocking on Demon's Door

Web of Desire

ABOUT CATHRYN

New York Times and *USA today* Bestselling author, Cathryn is a wife, mom, sister, daughter, and friend. She loves dogs, sunny weather, anything chocolate (she never says no to a brownie) pizza and red wine. She has two teenagers who keep her busy with their never ending activities, and a husband who is convinced he can turn her into a mixed martial arts fan. Cathryn can never find balance in her life, is always trying to find time to go to the gym, can never keep up with emails, Facebook or Twitter and tries to write page-turning books that her readers will love.

Connect with Cathryn:
Newsletter https://app.mailerlite.com/webforms/landing/c1f8n1
Twitter: https://twitter.com/writercatfox
Facebook: https://www.facebook.com/AuthorCathrynFox?ref=hl
Blog: http://cathrynfox.com/blog/
Goodreads: https://www.goodreads.com/author/show/91799.Cathryn_Fox

Pinterest http://www.pinterest.com/catkalen/

www.ingramcontent.com/pod-product-compliance
Lightning Source LLC
Chambersburg PA
CBHW021550310726
48972CB00003B/758